The Locater

The Story of a Super Computer

JAMES J. DOHERTY

authorHOUSE®

AuthorHouse™
1663 Liberty Drive
Bloomington, IN 47403
www.authorhouse.com
Phone: 1-800-839-8640

First published by AuthorHouse 1/27/2010

ISBN: 978-1-4389-8496-4 (sc)
ISBN: 978-1-4389-8497-1 (hc)

Printed in the United States of America
Bloomington, Indiana

This book is printed on acid-free paper.

PROLOGUE

The world is full of stories about missing persons. They are Family members, lost loved ones, old people, young people. They are people who seem to disappear from the face of the planet. People who are separated for one reason or another sometimes by adoption, kidnapping, amnesia. How sad it is to a mother who gives up her children for adoption because she couldn't support them, then years later regrets it. Heartbreaking is not the word for parents whose child is taken from them unlawfully and is either murdered or survives living with a new family.

Very often Investigators have to work with very little information Finding these people is occasionally pure luck, but with the advance of electronic science and the use of Computers, we have advanced to where no one will be invisible to law enforcement. Think of the advances that have been made in the just the last ten years. Think of what will be in the next thirty years. It will be beyond belief. This is a fictional story about an individual, who for good, attempts to help reunite people. He is a totally moral person. He asks no payment. He does not want fame or fortune. His satisfaction lies in that he has done good and that is all the payment he needs. He started with the basics of law enforcement and criminal investigations and then became part of the new process of modern science and the changing world of scientific criminal investigation.

ACKNOWLEDGMENT to: Denise Creighton, daughter of Geraldine and Robert Creighton distinguished members of the Smithtown community, Suffolk County Police Department, American Express and I could go on and on. Without Denise's help I could not have written this book and I sincerely wish to acknowledge her editing of the book.

CHAPTER I

The house is Victorian, with a wrap around porch. It has a small green lawn, meticulously kept. On top of the house are two towers. One on each side of the house. Inside the tower windows is the attic. The House was built by after the Civil War by a Confederate Admiral. He built the house for his bride. It was a very homey type home with 10 ft, ceilings and a marble fireplace in the living room. The house was left to Jim Feron and his wife. The man inside lives alone. His wife and children gone many years ago. They were kidnapped by a man, who he had arrested and was ultimately released, All attempts to find them living or dead were unsuccessful. The Locater had searched for fifteen years but no trace has been found. This tragedy motivated him to his present vocation. Finding people.

During the five years of his retirement he had helped to find thousands of people. When he retired from the New York City Police Department, he had reached the rank of Detective Sergeant in charge of an elite group of Detectives working on Organized Crime. He was about 6' tall and about 250 pound, his hair was thinner now but he still had pale blue eyes that were intimidating. His wife was a fresh faced home spun girl with a face like an angel. Her name was Elizabeth and she had originally come from a coal town in Pennsylvania he decided to go back to school and learn about computers. He studied hard and after eight long years he had learned as much as any school could teach him. It wasn't enough, though. They were leaving the church St. Mary's Roman Catholic church ,the church was an old style building with a beautiful altar and it had air conditioning, which made sitting at mass very comfortable. Jim's wife, Elizabeth and his son Jim and daughter Ann, four and three respectively went to Sunday mass and after parking the car and walking to the church the worst thing happened to them when they left church after mass. They paid no attention to the cars parked outside the church. The cars were parked by the people who were now going to the 11 o'clock Mass. Jim walked past the car, a black medium sized Ford with two men inside, who were watching the Ferons as they came down the marble steps of the church and walked to their car. They had no idea that they were about to be attacked. The street was crowded with families returning to their cars. Suddenly one man came out of the car. He approached Jim from behind. He was quick and strong. He grabbed Jim by the throat and brought him to the pavement. Another man was out of the car just as quickly and he ushered Elizabeth and the children into the Ford at gun point. It was a .38 Police Special. She desperately looked for her husband but he was on the ground, helpless. The man pushed a handkerchief soaked with ether into Jim's face and he was anesthetized. He had no idea that his family was being kidnapped. It all happened so fast that only one parishioner, Mrs .Mary Walsh. An eighty year old lady saw what was happening. The only problem was Mrs. Walsh could only see about five feet in front of her. Whenever she met Jim and his wife she had to be right on top of them to recognize them. By the time she was able to react and scream for help for anyone, the Ford was out of sight.

He spent the entire day into late evening talking to Detectives. He could not describe the man who came up behind him. Jim didn't even see his wife and children's plight .He was subdued almost immediately. The old lady gave a sketchy description of one of the kidnappers and all she knew was it was a black two door auto that they used. She did not know the make or model. After all she hadn't driven or bought a car in twenty years.

Detective Lieutenant Brown asked him a million questions, but it all boiled down to one theory. It could have been someone Feron had arrested who was now taking revenge against him. He finally went home, driven by one of the Squad Detectives. A young compassionate but rather helpless Detective. Jim would wait at the phone hoping that the kidnappers would contact him.

He sat by the phone until 5:00 AM but the phone didn't ring. He called his sister and his brother in law . They were his only family. Elizabeth's father was still alive and living in Donora, PA. He would not call him because the man was in his nineties and had a weak heart and he hoped that this nightmare would end before he would have to tell him. He certainly didn't need another tragedy on top of this one. The old man would certainly have a heart attack.

He spent every waking hour thinking. Could it have been Thomas Wilkens, the Serial Rapist, he put away and after six years escaped from prison? Was it John Tills, who had done five years for stealing from the bank he worked for? He went over every case he worked on over the last ten years. In his head he remembered sending a lot of crooks to jail. Some did not appear vindictive and yet some had given him that look when they left the court room after sentence.

The phone will ring he thought. What do they want? They have to want something and I have to prepare for it, he thought. Finally he dozed off and the phone did ring. He looked at the clock. It was 10 A.M. The call was from Lieutenant Brown. They had found a Ford, black, two door abandoned miles from the church. It had been stolen the day before. They believed that it could have been the car used in the kidnapping. Crime Scene Unit was going over the car with a fine tooth comb. He would get back to Jim if they found anything.

A few days later, he received a call. The voice said the words "No Nay, Never" then hung up It was part of an Irish ballad, however it seemingly was meant to mock . The call was traced to a phone booth not far from where the car was found.

Jim's mind raced back to an arrest he made of an Irish Terrorist, who was deported back to England for trial. He was responsible for several bombings in London and escaped to the United States where he was smuggling weapons when Jim caught the case and arrested him. He had heard that he escaped from Dart moor Prison in England and was never heard of again by Scotland Yard.

Could he have been the caller? Maybe?

Fifteen years later, Jim retired from the Police Department, never having heard a word about his missing family. Heartbroken, he never remarried or even took up with another woman. He went out with women. He took them to dinner, shows, movies for cocktails, but he never considered going any further . He never so much as kissed them good night. His partners considered him a weirdo but one or two of them who knew about his loss gave him as much support as they could.

Once away from the Police Department, he became a recluse. He seldom left his home until lone day he had an Epiphany. A neighbor and a close friend who lived a very blocks away approached him, Bill Stevens, was about fifty, and a very tall and handsome gentleman who worked in a bank for almost twenty years. He had known

Elizabeth and his kids and heard of his terrible loss and came over to his home one night. It had been a long time since Jim had lost his wife and children, however, the pain was still there. He was reluctant to welcome him in, however, something made him bid the man entrance. It was the look on the man's face. It was the kind of look he'd had, himself from that horrible day leaving Mass. The neighbor asked him if he still had contacts in the Police or did he know a good Private Investigator. His wife had died a year before and for many years she had talked about a twin sister that she had who was adopted by an aunt. The sister had gone with the aunt because the family was poor and could not support two children. His deceased wife's sister was never found. It was a long time scar that his wife bore. Now that she was dead, he wondered if maybe he could still find her. It would the closest thing to having his wife back, because she was a twin A crazy idea, he thought but maybe Mr. Feron could help him. Jim sat and listened to the man's story. Suddenly he thought if I help this man, perhaps it would in some way help him . He told his neighbor that he would do what he could. . He got as much information as he could about the missing sister and went to work using techniques that he had developed from years hunting down fugitives in the Police Department. Bill Stevens, Jim's neighbor gave him the aunt's name and their last known address at the time that the sisters were separated. He had heard that the aunt had remarried and moved out west. Jim went over the information and did some basic searches.

Out of town telephone listings, former neighbors still living who did not give any indications of her new identity or whereabouts proved futile, He was hitting brick walls. But here was a reason to go on. Bill's emptiness, the adrenaline rush Jim felt with each turn made him determined to push on. He would solve this mystery. Not only for Bill but for himself. He checked with the local parish for Marriage

Records. The first marriage was on record. A witness to the marriage was still living in the old neighborhood. He visited the witness. John Stone. He was a man of eighty, retired and suffering from an initial stages of Alzheimer so he wasn't to sharp. Jim questioned him for an hour or so and he was of little help until he mentioned that the aunt had worked for him in his hardware store and that's how they became friends and she had invited him and his wife to come to her Wedding in City Hall and be a witness. Jim asked him if he had any employment records. The old man feebly replied "I think I have some in the attic,but I don't know where". "You're free to look if you want"Jim left and Stone said that he would look in the attic some time later in the day. He had to have his lunch and his usual two hour nap afterwards.

When Jim got home he sat down and made himself a vodka martini. His version of a vodka martini was "Stoly" on the rocks with a twist and not a hint of Vermouth.

He had another "Stoly" and then dozed off. He slept dreaming of his wife and children and he remembered taking them all to Bermuda. They were on the beach at Achille Bay and the boy and girl who were good swimmers and were snorkeling, They were sandy haired kids, only a year apart and very athletic. Jim and Elizabeth sat comfortably, under an umbrella, sipping rum swizzles,occasionally glancing out at the kids to make sure they were all right.

The phone rang awakening him from his dream. He cursed, because it was such a pleasant memory and he did not want to let it go.

Stone had located an old 1099 IRS form with the name Jane Reynolds. It had a Social Security number and her old address. Jim immediately went to his Social Security Finder program on his computer. He punched in the Social Security number and there she was Jane Menton. She was living in Cape May in New Jersey. After a quick shower, he threw on his work clothes, a pair of jeans and a sports jacket that matched. He jumped into his car and drove. It would take him about three hours to get there. He enjoyed the ride even though it was on the turnpike and the only things along the way were oil refineries and corporate buildings. Once he got off the highway the scenery became a lot nicer. Farms and cows and horses.. He had been to Cape May once while in the job.

There was a prison there in Leesburg. He rolled into the town along Main Street. His map told him to make a left on Maple Street and another on Oak. Here it was Cedar Street and number 22. He pulled into the driveway. It was a Victorian style home with a white picket fence A neat clean house. A white haired woman in her fifties came out to see the stranger parking in her driveway. "Can I help you?" she said. "Are you Jane Menton?" She didn't answer but after a moment she answered "Yes it is. "I have been living with my aunt "She died a few years ago" "My husband and I lived with her."" Her name was Lucille West My husband is dead also." Do I know you?" Jim asked if they could go inside. She bid him in and became more friendly. "Bill Stevens had given him a picture of his wife and she could see the resemblance of her sister. He had found her. He then told her the story of his search for her. He proceeded very slowly trying his best not to upset her. She listened very intently and then tears came into her eyes. She put her head down and sobbed."I've wondered for so many years what had happened to my sister" she said through the sobbing. Then she became a combination of happy and sad. She was so thrilled that she could make contact with her sister's husband. She told Jim that she was widow and had no children and was very lonely. She was very active in her church and that was how she managed to battle her loneliness. Jim asked her if he could use her phone. He called Bill Stevens. When he told him the good news, he too started to cry and sob. He asked to talk to Jane. They talked and talked like they were long time friends. At this point Jim excused himself and started for the door. She jumped up, and put the phone down, telling Bill to hold on. She wrapped herself around Jim and asked him to stay. He told her he would be in touch. She looked into his eyes and with a look that expressed deep gratitude, she kissed him full on the lips. He turned and left. He had never had such a feeling of exultation in his life. He drove as if he were on a cloud. "The Locater" had been born.

There was a happy ending to this story because Bill Stevens and Lucille met went out to dinner a few times and then he asked her to marry him. She accepted and they were both very happy. He had a woman who so resembled his wife in every way. She had the same attributes of her sister so she immediately fell in love with Bill. Not all of "The Locater's" searches would end as happily as this.

CHAPTER II

He began his education anew in Computer Studies right after attending the wedding ceremony of Bill Stevens and Jane.

He enrolled in the Massachusetts Institute of Technology. He had to go through a process of gaining entrance, by producing his past high school education and the credits he received while in the Police Department. They even asked him to take an SAT test. He was interviewed and a few months later he was accepted. He rented a room and had his house boarded up with all of his and Elizabeth's furniture and personal belongings left inside. The house was not put up for sale. He would return, no matter how long after he completed his studies. He proved to be an apt pupil. He dove into his studies like a man possessed. His professor, Dr. Lermindov was extremely impressed with his student who took his course so seriously and intensely. Dr. Lermindov invited him for coffee one day after class. Lermindov was a middle aged professor and he was very smart. He spoke very good English with a slight Russian accent. He wanted to know more about this middle aged man who was his top student. He made the rest of the class look bad. They discussed the course at first but then the conversation drifted into family. Lermindov told how he got of Russia. He left during the cold war and it was very difficult for him. They did not take kindly to losing one of their top scientists to the west. His wife would not leave because she refused to leave her parents who she cared for They had no children. It was not all that hard for him to leave his wife since they had not gotten along and had not even slept together for the last five years. He stayed with her only because he felt obligated to help her and her parents who needed extra ordinary medical treatments and he could afford it because of his position as a scientist. Jim reluctantly told him of the loss of his wife and his long term career in the Police Department. He told him how he felt that computers would be the investigative tool of the future and how there was no limit to what the police would be able to do with the development of "super computers".Lermindov listened intently and you could see the wheels turning in his head as Jim spoke about how DNA would play a big part in investigations. How computers would be able to track missing persons or fugitives. How little pieces of evidence stored in a computer would eventually trap some killer. He was also impressed with this man's moral character which shone out like a beacon. This was a man of integrity and firm religious beliefs. He was jealous of him. He asked Jim what he was going to do once he completed the courses in Computer Science. Jim told him that he would study further and try to use his learning to help people. He had enough money through his pension to live comfortably and besides he would not take money for helping people. He had vowed not to. Lermindov decided that he wanted to help this man. He discussed private studies and then he told Jim of his "project". He had been involved privately in building a "super computer:" He had received some money in grants from the government and this with his own savings was funding his research. This would be "the computer to end all computers" Jim's eyes lit up. This sounded exciting and he wanted to be a part of it. A pact was agreed upon. The work would be a secret between them.

Alex Lermindov accepted Jim as his partner. Jim took money from an IRA an account that he opened years ago and agreed to contribute it to the project. It wasn't much in terms of a project of this magnitude but it helped. Lermindov hadn't accepted him as a partner for money. He liked Jim's ideas and listening to Jim's accounts of past investigations had made him a police buff. He did not realize when he started on his project that it would be so important to law enforcement as well as so many other fields. When he wasn't in class, Jim would be at Lermindov's side working on the "super computer" which he had nicknamed "Investicom".It was a huge machine with numerous dials and a printer. It was a "hackers dream"

Investicom was actually "hacking" everything it could get it's hands on. They hacked into Police Records, Medical Records, Funeral records, Birth Records, Death Records. All the records containing files of DNA, Fingerprints, Voice Analysis, Telephone Records. They hacked into Television News Files. The computer was storing an enormous amount of data.

About six months into the project, they decided to run a test. Jim had been watching John Walsh on "America's Most Wanted". They were looking for a child molester who had kidnapped two little girls and later they were found dead. His name was Herman Schwartz. He was a German national who emigrated to the United States and somehow Immigration had not picked up on his Interpol file of child abuse and molestation.

They showed a photo of him and in relating the story of his last kidnaping and killing, they mentioned that apparently one of the girls had either scratched him or bit him badly and he had seen a doctor in a small town outside of Hartford, Connecticut. The doctor after treating him for a "dog bite" asked the usual questions about the whereabouts of the animal. There would have to be a police report and a search of the animal for possible rabies or his patient would have to undergo painful treatment. The patient, Schwartz bolted out of the doctor's office and was seen driving away in a small pickup truck. After police were notified, identification was made of Schwartz, but he had escaped. A partial plate on the pick up truck only proved that it had been stolen. Lermindov and Feron tried" Investicom." They hacked into the medical records of the Hartford Medical Center and the Hartford Police Department. A blood sample was available as evidence of Schwartz's treatment for his "dog bite". The computer went to work and broke down the DNA of the blood sample. Now it was stored in the computer and then they ran a comparison with other collected DNA over the last year. Investicom hummed and clicked and went through it's data base. It would take about an hour for it to search. Lermindov and Jim went out to and had a Chinese dinner at a local restaurant. They ate rather quickly, both of them eager to get back to Lermindov's laboratory and see what if anything "Investicom" had discovered.

As they entered the lab, the printer was printing out pages of data. The report was about twenty pages. First a match was made early in the year, before the kidnapping at a doctor's office in New Haven, A patient, by the name of of H. Schultz had gotten a blood test. He gave an address, which later turned out to be false. He did however use a Social Security Number on his doctor's application. The SSN registered to a Henry Schmitt. The latest check on this SSN showed an application for work in Harrisburg, Pennsylvania. Schmitt had applied for work as a lawn maintenance worker at a private religious school for children. He was stalking his latest victims. Feron called the number for "Americas Most Wanted" which was regularly given on the program. He got a polite receptionist who he told that he might have information as to the whereabouts of Schwartz. She switched his call to a hot line number operated by the FBI. An agent took down the information but kept asking him how he knew that Schwartz was in Harrisburg Jim could not tell him and also refused to identify himself so the agent refused to take the information from him. Exasperated he hung up and called the Harrisburg Police. He spoke with the Chief and this time he explained that he was a retired Police Officer from New York and that he had an old informant who knew Schwartz and gave him his present location. The Chief asked for a number where he get back to him and Jim gave him the general number of the university. Several hours later, the phone rang in Lermindov's apartment above the laboratory. It was Harrisburg's Chief. He was excited. They had captured Schwartz. The press was all over him. He wanted to know if he could tell them about Jim's information. "No, Definitely not", he said. The Chief pleaded with him, but Feron insisted that his identity remain a secret. He told the Chief that it would jeopardize the safety of his informant. He gave all the excuses, he could think of.

The next day, the story broke and unfortunately, the Chief had given the press the story of how he received information from a retired New York City Police Officer, who was now attending MIT. Lermindov and Jim decided that this was a time to take a sabbatical. The class was over except for Term Papers which were required by the students for a final grade. Lermindov made arrangements with the university to have the papers graded by an associate, who he would keep in touch with. The evaluation of the papers would be faxed to a number he would give his associate. He got the Dean to agree to let him go. He told him that it was a family emergency that had to be taken care of. Jim and Alex boarded a plane for London and avoided a confrontation with the press. They were told that Feron, who had been a student had gone on vacation to a location unknown to the university.

CHAPTER IV

The trip to London was wonderful. Jim and Alex thoroughly enjoyed visiting the Tower of London, the Palace, Madame Tussaud's Museum and a trip to Scotland Yard which was arranged through friends of Jim's in the "job". The job of course being the New York City Police Department. They went out one night with couple of the inspectors and exchanged war stories of investigations they were involved in. The Scotland Yard Detectives were very interested in investigations conducted in New York. Their admiration for NYPD was very obvious. They were no slouches themselves and their methods interested both Jim and Alex.

One of the Scotland Yard Inspectors had been born in Scotland and he recommended that Jim and Alex take a little trip up to St. Andrews, play a little golf and enjoy the Scottish countryside. They rented a car and started north. They were not disappointed. When they got to St. Andrews, there was an amateur golf tournament going on and it was being played despite wind gusts of up to 40 miles an hour. They both stood on the side street from which you could observe the 18th hole and watched as balls flew crazily in the winds sometimes coming very close to where they were standing. There was a hotel about a block away from the course, which had a nice little restaurant so they decided to have lunch and make reservations for an overnight stay before traveling further north.

The restaurant had typical Scottish fare such as sausage, black pudding, meat pies, Steak and Kidney pie and Bangers and Mash. The hostess greeted them at the door and asked if they were just two for lunch. She led them past some tables to a table in the rear which had a window overlooking the golf course. As they sat down, Jim noticed two very pretty women, who looked like they had obviously played golf very early and were now settling down for a nice lunch. They had their clubs tucked in the corner near their table. Jim could not help staring at the one woman who resembled his wife and he knocked over his glass of water because he kept staring. Alex asked him "What's wrong, Jim?" He said "Nothing". Alex said "You looked like you saw a ghost." Jim smiled a queer smile and said "Maybe I just did". The one woman couldn't help noticing the gentlemen to her left particularly the one who kept looking over at them. On one of his glances their eyes met and she smiled politely back at him. They were close enough to speak and she said "Americans?" and he nodded. "And how did you hit them today?" he said to her. "Oh, I'm terrible, Elaine here, she is a pro. She broke a 100." Jim felt bold enough to ask the ladies to join them for an after dinner drink and to his surprise they agreed. They all sat together at Jim and Alex's table and Alex seemed to enjoy the ladies company as much as Jim did. They introduced each other. The women were Elaine and the one that resembled Jim's wife was Anne. No last names were given. They had a couple of Drambuies and everyone chatted about America and Scotland and a lot of small talk about golf and St. Andrews. Jim could not take his eyes off of her. She was enchanting and had a cute little Scottish accent. He made fun of it a couple of times and she took his kidding and returned it with a distorted New York accent. She used words like "Long Giland" and "bottle" like a typical New Yorker. They laughed and he asked "What are you doing for dinner?" "Nothing" she said and She agreed to meet him for dinner, but Elaine and Alex recognizing the situation both declined with a wink. They wanted the two to have an evening alone.

They met later in the lobby and walked into the bar and ordered a couple of drinks. She had changed into a black evening dress and he had put on a sports jacket and slacks. They looked very smart and made for an attractive couple. People stared at them as they entered the bar. He ordered his usual a "Stoly" on the rocks with a twist and she had an Amaretto Sour.

"Are you married?" she asked as she looked at the gold band on his finger. "I was, but I believe that she is dead." "I don't understand?" "Did she leave you?" "It's a long Story. She was kidnapped about fifteen years ago and we never found her." She wanted to change the subject, but he related the story of the abduction in front of the church and his long time search with out any results. He had a forlorn look about him as he told her of his personal tragedy. She reached over and held his hand. He was about to fall in love. She had such a sympathetic way about her, He thought. It was uncanny, how much she reminded him of his wife. Same well scrubbed face. She actually didn't need makeup. Lovely blue eyes and a trim figure He asked her if she was married and she said "Almost" "I even bought the gown, but he chickened out at the last moment." "What a fool." he said. The both laughed. "But, you know I'm glad that he did." "You are." she said with her mouth open. "Sure, if you were married, I probably wouldn't be sitting here having a drink with the most charming woman I've met since I lost my wife." She was flattered and her face flushed a little. They had another drink and then the hostess led them to a table. They lingered at the table after dinner and chatted and she sipped a glass of Amaretto while he cradled a B&B. He found that they had a lot in common. She liked to play golf and he had taken it up since retirement. He could tell she liked children from the way she looked at them in the dining room. A little tousled haired girl was leaving with her Mom and Dad and dropped her stuffed animal. Anne quickly retrieved it and handed to her with a smile. The little girl just looked and her mother said "What do you say?" "Thank you" she said. Anne sneezed a couple of times and remarked that she thought she had caught a cold from the cold winds on the golf course. "God Bless You" said Jim and offered his handkerchief. She took it and then returned it to him. He just tucked it in his pocket. "I must be getting to bed, We have an early day tomorrow and this cold is not helping things." Jim sadly said "Yeah, Alex and I going up to the Isle of Skye in the morning," "Oh, you'll love it up there" said Anne. "Will you still be here in St. Andrews when we come back?" he asked. "When are you coming back". "Day after tomorrow, We are just going for the day." "Oh we will be here until then, but then our holiday is over." said Anne. He was happy that she would still be here when he returned. He wanted to see her again very badly. Jim and Alex got up at Dawn and had a quick breakfast in the lounge. They just had juice, coffee and a roll and then they were on the way up north to the Isle of Skye The trip took them about eight hours. They stopped along the way and had lunch at a little pub. A pint of ale and some Bangers went down well. When they got to the Bridge of Orchy, they stopped at a hotel and stayed the night before going on to Skye. Jim was very quiet most of the trip and Lermindov studied his expression. "Penny for your thoughts, Jim" Jim said "Oh just thinking about St. Andrews." "Want to go back?" Lermindov asked. "Nah, lets finish our trip." Then he suddenly looked at Alex and said "Alex, Would you mind if we went back?"Alex knew why he wanted to go back. They agreed to sleep over at the Bridge of Orchy and travel back early the next morning.

The rented car they were using sat outside the hotel facing in. While they had their breakfast, they heard a loud crash outside. Jim went to the window and saw a garbage truck had backed into the side of their car. It had hit part of the radiator and fluid from the radiator was pouring out onto the parking lot. Alex and Jim went outside and the truck driver apologized profusely to both of them after learning that it was their auto that he hit. A local policeman responded to the scene and started on the necessary paper work. In the mean time Jim went to the desk of the hotel to find out about another rental. There was only one rental agency nearby and they wouldn't have any vehicles until the next day. Jim and Alex would have to stay another day.

The next day they waited for the call from the Car Rental Agency but the morning passed and no call. Jim called them again and was told there would be a car delivered to the hotel by noon. Noon came and still no car. He paced up and down in front of the hotel and the decided to go in to the pub and have a drink with Alex.

The car was finally delivered, however it was not until after 3 o'clock. They packed up their gear and started back to St. Andrews. Without any stops they got back about ten in the evening. Jim immediately called Anne's room but there was no answer. The desk clerk informed him that the ladies had left just before tea time. "Did they leave any messages?" "Wait I think the one lady left you a message." He unfolded the piece of paper and read her note."Jim, I am so sorry that we could not have had another dinner together, Elaine and I had to leave a little early, Her mother is not well. We are going on to Glasgow. If you would like to call me my cell phone is 555-6789. Oh by the way my last name is Fulton. I look forward to your call. I hope you and Alex had a nice trip up north. Love Anne.

CHAPTER V

Their holiday was almost over. They would travel back to Glasgow, stay overnight and then catch a British Airways Flight back to the United States. Jim actually was happy that the trip was over because he would be going to Glasgow and could see Anne again. He got a disappointment though. Anne had accompanied Elaine to Edinburgh to help her in getting her mother into a nursing home. She would not be back until his departure date. They spoke for three hours on the telephone and then they both reluctantly hung up. It was 2 o'clock in the morning. Anne said she would try to get to the airport to have a farewell drink with him and he said "Please be there." She promised that she would.

The check in at the airport was long. Their bags and ticket verifications were finished. They were assigned their seats and told what gate to pass through. Jim stayed outside of the metal detector as long as he could so that he could still have that farewell drink with Anne. The time though was getting short and Alex nervously reminded him that they should pass through the gate to the plane entrance.

Anne got out of the taxi in front of the airport departure entrance. She was not paying attention to what was going on around her. Her eyes searched for the British Airways information desk. She glanced up and saw on the TV monitor that Flight 111 was leaving at 5:10 PM. It was now 5:09. She ran towards the metal detector entrance. Unfortunately she didn't see the Red Cap with the large baggage cart. He tried to avoid her but he couldn't and crashed into her. She hit the floor hard and her purse went flying.

He was one of those characters who roams around railroad stations and airports looking for opportunities to steal luggage. A "skel " (a term used by the Police for a low life or petty thief) When the purse flew right to his feet, he leaned down and picked it up. No one was looking. He put it under his coat and went directly to the Men's room. In one of the stalls, he went through the purse and found the usual ladies makeup, comb and lipstick. There was a wallet tucked inside and this is what he was really after. He dropped the purse and inside the wallet was $120 and some change. There were two credit cards and an identification folder. "Nice haul" he said to himself and quickly left the bathroom and then walked slowly out of the airport. He got on a bus, which was waiting to go to London sat by the open window and slowly dropped the credit cards and the identification folder out of the window as the bus moved out of the airport parking area, meanwhile Anne who was unconscious lay waiting for an ambulance. One soon arrived and before it left an officer arrived to take a report. "No Id on her", said the ambulance driver. "We'll have to wait to talk to her when she comes to to find out who she is.

No one could know that she would suffer from a rare form of amnesia and not be able to identify herself.

The jet rose quickly from the tarmac. Below, the Tower Bridge could be seen. Jim sat quietly with his hand to his head. "Headache?" asked Alex. "No, I'm alright" and then he leaned back and closed his eyes. He slept and dreamed. He was back in Bermuda with Anne this time. They were having a glass of wine together at the "Wharf Restaurant". This was a restaurant on the dock of St. George. A cruise ship was right in front of them, big and beautiful. He asked her if she was having a good time and she smiled and said "I'm having such a wonderful time and I can't tell you how much I'm enjoying my new name Anne Fulton Feron. I've never been so happy and they clinked their glasses.

CHAPTER VI

They were soon back at MIT and in the laboratory. Jim could not wait to call Scotland to find out why Anne did not come to the airport. At first he just got the answering machine and then after a few more calls, the machine was full and didn't work right. He dove into the research that Alex and he were working on. "Investicom" had grown so much that more space was needed . This was a problem for them to work out. The memory part of the computer had to be expanded. The information that they were storing was coming in faster and faster.

After a week of twelve hour days, Alex suggested that Jim take a break and check on his house, which had been closed up since he started at MIT. Jim was tired and decided that he would check on the "old shack" as he called it. He packed up an overnight bag and was about to leave when he got an idea that he would call Scotland one more time. This time a human voice answered. It was Elaine. She was excited to hear from Jim, but she had bad news. "Anne has disappeared." she said. "What do you mean "disappeared" " "She left to go to the airport and I haven't heard from her since." "Did she see you off?" "No, she never got there on time as far as I know." Jim now was almost frantic. "She didn't call or come home." "I thought maybe the two of you had eloped." She laughed nervously. "Now, I"m really worried about her." "I'm going to call the police." Jim suggested that she go there and bring photos of Anne and also call one of the Inspectors in Scotland Yard that he had made the acquaintance of, who might have some ideas of where to start looking for her. His name was Hector Thomson. He had deja vu of the time when his wife was kidnapped. It couldn't happen to him twice, he thought. "I have to go to Long Island for a day, here is my telephone number there. If I'm not there, please leave a message and let me know as soon as you find out something, please, please."

Before he got home, he called the telephone company and told them to reactivate his telephone, which had been shut down while he was away. He got to the house and walked into a musty smelling living room. He opened all of the windows and left the door open. While he was doing this, the phone rang. He quickly picked it up. It was the phone company testing that his phone was not working. He had hoped it was Elaine. He sat down in his lounge chair and made himself a vodka and waited.. It was like the night he lost his wife, sitting in that chair waiting for the phone to ring. The phone rang again. This time it was Alex. They had received a grant from the government to pursue their project with "Investicom". Alex somberly asked Jim "Have you heard anything about Anne "Nothing yet."

Jim shopped at a local King Kullen in Bay Shore, L.I. On this particular day, he stopped for a drink at "Tellers", a restaurant on Main Street. Gerry the bartender asked him how he was and how his studies were going. Little did he know of the heavy burden that Jim was carrying at the time and Jim didn't want to talk about it even though a bartender is usually a sounding board for all sorts of problems. Jim had his "stoly" and went to the super market. He went down the aisles picking up some bread, eggs, bacon, soda and then as an after thought he picked up a six pack of beer. He got on the checkout line which had two people ahead of him. He just got a glimpse of a man in his forties, with a bandanna , jeans and a rather long pony tail, who was at the front of the line. Next in line was a slight woman, about seventy with Grey hair, who was having difficulty putting her purchases on the checkout track. He helped her and she turned and smiled. "Lovely day, isn't it" she said. "Yes, ma'am" and Jim stepped up to the back of the line. The man with the bandanna was helping the cashier put his groceries in bags. He was humming a song, which sounded familiar to Jim. Then he said the words, softly as he bagged. "No Way never, never no more.." The veins in Jim's neck swelled as the blood rushed to his head. Their eyes met and the man stopped bagging and slowly backed away from the counter. First he started walking slowly away without his groceries. "Hey, where are you going said the cashier." Then he took off toward the door. Jim at first tried to push past the old lady, then he backed up and went out the next aisle, which was unattended. He was after him as fast as his legs could carry him. The man went out the door and sprinted into the parking lot. He had about a twenty yard lead on Jim. He got to a pickup truck and burned rubber going out of the lot. Jim got to his car and peeled off after him. They raced west on Montauk Highway toward the small town of Bay Shore. Which was less than a quarter mile away. As the pickup truck climbed the hill that came into town, it came up behind a passenger car, which was stopped at the traffic light. He had no way to go around it. Jim was seconds behind him. He jumped out of the truck and started running up Main Street . Jim had to abandon his car also, because he too was stuck behind the passenger car. He was well behind the man and all he could do was maintain the distance between them. As the man approached an intersection he ran left down toward the ferry slip. There was a ferry slip which took vacationers to Fire Island. It was a long run down the avenue to the slip and Jim was losing ground, however, he maintained a visual on the man. Every now and then, the man looked back to see where Jim was. It took Jim another minute to get to the ferry slip, just in time to see it pulling away. He got a glimpse of a man with a bandanna looking out of the window of the ship towards him. He cursed his unfitness. In his younger days he would have caught the man easily. Was this man connected in any way with the disappearance of his wife? The man had a full mustache and his head was covered but he was about 5'9" and maybe 165 pounds. He was muscular and fit. Jim would have to search his mind as to who in his past investigations fit this description. He went to a phone and called the Fire Island Constable. He got a young man who was a summer replacement. He told the young man to look out for a man with a bandanna getting off of the ferry that had just departed from Bay Shore. "Why?" and "Who are you." he asked. Jim explained that he was a retired police officer and that the man was wanted for questioning. The summer fill in said "I can't do that without a warrant." "Besides, I'm assigned to giving summonses for taking food onto the beach." Frustrated , Jim asked for a supervisor. "He is over at "Flynn's"(a local restaurant) "There is a drunk over there causing trouble." Finally, Jim gave up and went back to his car, which he had pulled rather quickly, before he set out on foot after "Mr. Bandanna" Jim drove to the 3rd Precinct Detective Squad, where he met Steve Gargan an old friend of his. He related the story to him of his chase and Steve listened intently. He knew Jim wasn't some hack that had chased a "hippy" with a bandanna for no good reason. Steve suggested that that they go back to the store and get their video tape which would identify "Mr. Bandanna" Steve would call the chief in Fire Island and ask him to have his men look out for a man fitting the description that Jim gave him. They both figured that "Mr. Bandanna" would find a way to leave the island soon after he got there and they were right because later a small boat was reported stolen from the island and abandoned on the Captree side of the bay, which was on the side of the island that Jim had lost him initially.

One good thing came out of it though, Steve got the video tape and Jim was able to pick out "Mr. Bandanna" They got a nice full face photo from the tape. Jim recognized an old "collar" from fifteen years ago. He went back to the house and opened a drawer which was full of photos and "yellow sheets." Yellow sheets was police jargon for a police record. There it was, Brian Ferguson. Jim had locked him up as a group of IRA terrorists. They had a cache of guns and dynamite, which were found during the execution of a Search Warrant. Brian was one of the group and through the aid of a smart lawyer, he got off because he said he was just visiting his friends when the arrest was made and the jury believed him. He did give Jim the evil eye as he left the court room and mumbled "I'm gonna fix your ass, copper."

Brian had fallen off the face of the earth afterward and had not been heard from in police circles. Jim thanked his friend and told him he would be going back to MIT and if Steve heard anything more about Ferguson, he could be reached there

CHAPTER VII

Alex looked tired and pale when Jim came into the laboratory. "Didn't you take a break yourself." said Jim. "I've been working on expanding the memory of "Investicom" and I had a few glitches that I cleaned up also." "Everything is good now." "I am going up to my room and lie down, the old Grey mare ain't what it used to be." Alex left for his room but before he did he went over to Jim and hugged him and gave him a kiss on the cheek. "Anything exciting in Bay Shore, Jim?" "No it's a very quiet town." Jim didn't want to go into his adventure with Alex right now. When he was well rested he'd tell him everything.

Vito D'Angelo, sat at the corner table overlooking Mulberry and Hester Streets in lower Manhattan in the area known as "Little Italy" because of all the Italians and Italian Americans that lived there. Vito was a semi-retired "Capo" and he had taken the name Vito. His real name was Victor. Because he admired Vito Genovese so much he changed his name to Vito. He was rumored to have been a "Counsigieri" with one of the Crime Families and. Also rumored to have done a couple of murders. He was reading an article in the N.Y. Times that had caught his interest."Professor and Retired Detective receive Government grant of $250,000 to help them in their research project involving a super secret computer that will might help enable law enforcement in locating missing persons." His eyes lit up and his summoned one of his "Soldiers". "Tony did you ever run into this Jimmy Feron?" Tony stood silent for a moment and then said "I think he's the one that locked up group of our guys for a hi-jack job from the airport." "What kind of guy is he "Unfortunately an honest cop." "We couldn't buy him off." "He treated our guys decently though, no rough stuff." "Hmm, I want to talk to you about something I may want him to do." "Do you think he would take a job from me, even though it's legit?" " I don't think so boss. He doesn't take to associating with any of the family members." "Well, I want you to try him anyway."

Jim and Alex weren't happy over the article in the paper. It meant that they would have to move their equipment from the University complex. Too many people now knew that they were working on something very valuable. They had to consider the security of the project. All of the computer equipment was trucked out to a secret location in Long Island, where an old airport hanger was still standing from a deserted Aircraft Company. It just looked like and abandoned warehouse. The building had a basement which was not visible from the outside. The top floor just looked like an abandoned hanger. A secret door led to the basement. The computer was left in crates outside the building and Jim and Alex took the crates on hand trucks through the secret door that had a runway leading to the basement. They took the crates down the runway and there they would assemble"Investicom" again. Jim and Alex then parted company. Jim went back to his home and Alex to his apartment located on the campus of MIT. Alex would have to find an apartment in Long Island now so he could be close to "Investicom." They would meet at the hanger every day and there they reassembled

"Investicom" Both of them were very careful to make sure that they were not surveilled in their travels from the two locations. It took them weeks to reassemble the computer, but they both were satisfied that it was safer now.

Jim was home on a weekend relaxing. He and Alex were taking the weekends off now."All work and no play." Alex would say. He was having his morning coffee when the bell rang. A big burly man stood at the door. "Feron?" he said.

"Who are you?" Jim said very curtly. "And, What do you want?"

"Don't get testy, I'm here on behalf of a friend. He's heard all about you and wants you to find someone for him, We'll make it worth your while." "I'm not interested."

"Wait, wait until I tell you how much he's willing to pay." "It could match the money you got in your government grant." "I'm still not interested." he said.

"Look, I know all about you. I know your reputation for being an honest cop."

"This man wants to find his daughter." "It's very important to him and he thinks maybe you can do it."Jim became curious. "Who is the man, who wants to find his daughter?" "Mr. Vito D'Angelo.""And you think I would work for him?"said Jim. "Why don't we take a ride to the city and let him tell you himself what he wants you to do." "Okay?" Jim thought to himself."If I could do something for a crime family member what would he be willing to give me in return besides money." He got in the car with the burly man who identified himself as "Dom".

They drove along the Long Island Expressway to the Brooklyn Queens Expressway which led to the Williamsburg Bridge and Manhattan.The car turned onto the Bowery and then turned into

Hester Street. It pulled up in front of Umbriano's restaurant. They went in and sat down at a table where Vito sat alone staring out the window. He had a twenty dollar Cuban Cigar in his mouth and he puffed and puffed big rings of smoke. He looked up and waived Jim into a chair at his table. He extended his hand and introduced himself. "I know who you are." said Jim."I don't know that I want this kind of action." "Don't start making a decision before you hear what I have to say." "I have or had a daughter. She was only eighteen. Should be about 23 now." "I had plans for her to marry someone with class and not connected with the family. She fell for a kid down the block. He worked in the Deli on the corner. Not very impressive." "She wanted my blessing so they could get married. I said no. First she was too young and what kind of prospects did this kid have." "The next I know they're gone." "I found out they got married in City Hall under a different name."" I haven't been able to find them for five years." "Listen, Detective Feron, I found out recently that I have Cancer and I've got maybe a year. Six months of decent living before I wind up with tubes in me." " I want you to find them for me." "Why? So you can mess up the kid?" said Jim. "No, I swear I won't touch him. As a matter of fact I want them to get married proper in the church and I want a nice reception." "What guarantees do I have that you won't harm either one of them?" "I swear on my mother's grave." Jim laughed. "I just passed your mother the other day on Ocean Parkway. She was sitting on the stoop outside her house." " She looked pretty healthy to me." Vito chuckled "I was just testing you." "You know I have a nephew who is a priest. He is assigned to St. Anthony's over here on Sullivan Street.""If you want we can over there and I will swear on one of his bibles that what I say is true.""Never mind. Vito, your word is all I want."

"But if anything ever happens to those kids, I'll see to it that you spend your last year or years in Attica prison." "You have a hidden interest in a Computer Manufacturer. They are involved in a lot of research. My partner and I need parts for our computer. We sometimes have to wait weeks to get these parts. Also your engineers can create parts for us built to our specifications. That's what I want from you." "You got it." said Vito.

Vito gave Jim all the information he could about his daughter and her lover. They were married sometime in the Spring, maybe May of 1996. They got married in City Hall. Vito gave Jim his daughter, Angela's date of birth. He didn't know her husband's. He guessed that he was about two years older than her. Jim had all sorts of medical records of Angela and of course photos but no fingerprints. She of course had never been arrested. Jim had her DNA from blood tests that she'd had during her young life. He went to "Investicom" and put the computer to work. He found a match on the DNA. Blood tests taken by couples applying for Marriage Licenses. Angela Contino applied with an Anthony Pinto.

Once he had the names, it was easy for him to find out that a marriage was performed a couple of days later in the chapel in City Hall between Angela and Anthony. Anthony gave a Social Security Number on the application.

A check of the Social Security number revealed that an Anthony Contino had lived in Washington, Pennsylvania up to a year ago. It gave an address of 12 Pike Street. Jim got in his car and proceeded toward Washington. As he passed over the Verrazano Bridge and south toward the New Jersey Turnpike, he noticed a car behind him making the same kind of moves that he did. When he got to one of the gas stops on the Turnpike, he pulled off and went into the cafeteria. The car behind him pulled in also. He went into the gift shop from which he was able to see the entrance to the cafeteria. Two men came in and they looked left and right. One headed for the Men's room and the other searched the sit down area of the cafeteria. Jim ducked out behind the one man who was looking in the cafeteria. He headed for their car. When he got to the car he took the cap off of the air valve on one of the tires. He stuck a wooden match into it and watched the air escape from the tire and then he got in his car and left. Once in the car he dialed his cell phone. He had a speaker on his phone so it was hands free. He called "Umbrianos" "Let me speak toVito." "Vito not here." "Who's calling." "Listen "Goomba" tell Vito that Jimmy Feron is on the phone." The next voice was unmistakably Vito. "What's up?" he said. "You listen to me, Mr. D'Angelo. Get your boys off of my back. If I see them tailing me again, I'll drop the case." "I have a pretty good lead and your men are fucking things up. Do I make myself clear?" "It won't happen again." said Vito.

Vito was true to his word. When his men came out of the cafeteria and found that they had a flat tire, they called "Umbrianos" and were told to come back. They fixed the tire and returned to New York. Jim rolled into Washington after an eight hour ride. It was late so he found a Motel and checked in for the night. There was a State Store still open so he bought himself a bottle of "Stoly" poured a couple of stiff ones and went to bed.

He got up early and found a local diner where he had his breakfast. Then he drove to 12 Pike Street. He knocked on the door and young girl with an infant came to the door. It was not Angela. She told Jim and she and her husband had recently bought the house from a young man with a four year old girl . She didn't know where they had moved to. The man's name was Contino. There was no woman. The girl thought that perhaps the man had divorced or separated from his wife and was a single parent. Jim went to the local Post Office to see if Contino's left a forwarding address. The Postmaster would not give out that information. Jim told him that he was a retired Detective from New York, but the Postmaster still wouldn't give out the information. Jim went out into the street and there was a carrier just about to drive away. Jim approached him and asked him if he delivered to Pike Street. "Yeah, that's on my route." "Do you remember a family Contino?" "Oh yeah, young guy with a little girl. ." "Where did they move to?" "I'm not supposed to give out that information, sir." "This man is related to someone important and it would mean a lot to him if I could find him." "Look here is my retired NYPD badge, I wouldn't bullshit you." "They moved to Mentor, Ohio." 2115 Madison Street. "Thanks buddy" Jim offered the carrier a twenty. "No thanks officer." "I wish you luck." "My dad was a cop in Pittsburgh. He was killed on the job. That was ten years ago.""God rest him" said Jim and shook the carriers hand.

It took Jim another four hours to reach Mentor and Madison Street. There was no one home, so he sat in his car outside the house and read the local paper. He had almost finished the crossword when a car pulled into the driveway. A young man with a little girl. He got out of the car and walked toward them. The man turned and sensing something, started to run away from the house. Of course he couldn't run very fast carrying the little girl and Jim caught him easily. He took a swing at Jim but Jim ducked and grabbed his arm. The little girl was on the ground and she was crying. "Wait, I'm not here to hurt you." "Lets talk." said Jim. He finally got Anthony calmed down enough to listen to him. "I don't want any part of Mr. D'Angelo or his kind." "My wife is dead. I lost her last year. All I have left is our little girl. I just want to be left alone." Jim tried to convince him that nothing would happen to either one of them if they went back to

New York. "If he could just see his little grand daughter, I know he'd be satisfied.""No, I know his kind. Control is all they know.""Okay, how about this. I call him up and tell him that his daughter passed away, but he has a grand daughter." "I'll send him a picture. I won't tell him where you are." "Would you agree to that?" "How do I know I can trust you?" Tony said sternly. "I really can't give you a guarantee except that I would do everything in my power to see that you are treated right." "Look, your name is Anthony, here is My medal of St. Anthony, your namesake. . He has seen me through a lot in my life." He smiled. Something about his smile made Anthony feel at ease and he reluctantly got a bag packed and prepared to accompany Jim back to New York. Jim prepared Vito for the shock of the death of his daughter by telephoning him from Ohio. Vito was excited that Jim had been but when he heard Jim's tone change he knew something was wrong "Tell me the worst." he said. Jim talking softly and slowly told Vito that his daughter had contracted breast cancer and was dead. "What about the husband?""He's here he's still afraid of you." Jim could hear the slow sobbing coming over the phone. Vito managed to control himself and then he said "Tell Anthony to come back, I wouldn't harm him. Angela would roll over in her grave." Jim then told him about the grand child.. "You mean I have a little grand daughter," "What does she look like. I"ll bet she looks like Angela."Please hurry back, no wait take your time, I wouldn't want you to get into an accident. I'll be waiting here for you, no matter how late you get back."When Jim, Anthony and his little girl got back to New York and pulled up in front of "Umbriano"'s it was about ten o"clock. The little girl was asleep and Anthony cradled her in his arms as they entered the restaurant. Vito was standing waiting for them. He walked over and took his grand daughter in his arms and as he did she woke up. She looked up at him with those beautiful blue eyes and snuggled her head on his shoulder. She was a beautiful blond haired little girl. He started to cry.

She was starting to be more alert now and she said "Daddy, I'm hungry." "What do you want?" Vito asked."How about some spumoni?" He summoned a waiter and in minutes she had her spumoni. "What's her name?" he asked Anthony. "Angela, after her mother." "Oh Thank you God I've got my little Angela back again." Vito then hugged Anthony and told him that he wanted to help both of them "I know how you feel about me, but for Angela's sake, let me help you." Anthony nodded and this is when Jim felt it was time for him to go. "Wait where are you going, I have to settle with you." and he pulled out a wad of cash. "You don't owe me anything, maybe a little gas money, but consider it a gift. So long Mr. D"Angelo, Good Luck Anthony, Goodbye sweetheart." He patted little Angela on the head and went out the door. "Sucker" mumbled Vito but he never respected anyone as much as he did Jim at that moment.

Anthony who had attended Stuyvesant High School as a Science Major and had always wanted to be a doctor became one with Vito's help. Vito bought them a little house in Massapequa, Long Island, which had a big back yard. He would come out on the weekends to be with his grand daughter. He drove out himself without "his goon bodyguards". After a few months Anthony recognized the symptoms of the disease Vito was carrying and invited him to sleep over. Vito would stay on the weekends until Monday and leave late in the morning so he would not hit any traffic.

It lasted like this for about six months when Anthony got a call that Vito was in New York University Hospital. The end was near. He took Angela in to see her grandfather a couple of times and then he stopped. It was not a pretty sight seeing the old man die. He made one last trip and told Vito he would not be coming in again. Vito agreed and gave his "little Angela" a hug and a kiss. "Grab tight." she said She was told by Anthony to kiss her grand father because they had to go. She did and gave him a little wave as they walked out the door. Vito closed his eyes and went to sleep to dream about playing with his daughter in happier days. He died a week later.

CHAPTER VIII

Jim went back to his house in Bay Shore and there was a message on his answering machine from Hector Thomson. He said he had found Anne in a nursing home in Edinburgh. It was the "Shady Rest Home" An aide had taken her prints when she arrived as an unidentified person and sent them down to headquarters. A match was made. Anne had applied for a government job when she was about eighteen and that's how the match was made. Thomson was notified because he had put her name in their system. He was going up to Edinburgh and wanted Jim to know. He would call him when he got back. Jim couldn't wait. He booked a flight to Edinburgh for the next day.

Alex got a call from Jim telling him that he would be gone for a couple of days and that they had found Ann. Alex told him"Go for it." "Call me when you know more." Alex went back to work in the laboratory.

Alex was in the laboratory deep into a project when the phone rang. He answered it immediately thinking it was probably Jim. A voice came on that he didn't recognize., "Is Jim Feron there?" It had a distinct Irish brogue. "No, he's not here right now, who is calling." "Tell him that an old friend called and I didn't like Fire Island that much, too many "faggots". Alex knew who it was. He wanted to keep him on the phone as long as he could. He put "Investicom"into operation to trace the call. Then he started a new program which he and Jim and incorporated into the computer. It was a voice operated system. It worked like this. They had put their voice into a program. The program knew their voice and it knew their personality. The program could conduct a conversation with someone with their voice and the way that they would answer certain questions or ask questions so that the person on the other line thought that they were actually talking to either Jim or Alex. Alex hit the switch and his voice and personality took over the conversation. He wanted to delay the caller so he could find out where the call was coming from. Bingo, "Investicom" located the caller as being only a mile and a half down the road on Route 110 at a "Dunkin Donuts" The caller was wise and said "Don't think that you can trace this call in time to catch me." "I used to work for the phone company and I know how long it takes to trace a call." Alex then said "Oh wait a minute Jim just came in. Here he is." The caller could not resist the opportunity to taunt his pursuer. Alex switched on the computer system which had Jim's voice and personality and then ran out the door to his car. He drove south on Route 110 and spotted the Dunkin Donuts shop on the north side of the highway. He had to drive a little further south so he could turn around and nearly crashed into a truck while he made his "U" Turn. As he pulled into the parking lot of the Dunkin Donuts, a young man was exiting with a container of coffee in his hand. He had a pony tail and Alex knew just then that this is "the guy" He walked up to the man and asked him " How do I get to Amityville?" "You turn around and go south said "Pony Tail." and then got into his van. Alex thanked him and walked a few feet away and then pivoted and stuck a revolver in the window and put it up against "Pony tail'" head.

"Don't move" he said. "What is this?" said "Ponytail". "Give me that Cell phone there on the dash." "Pony tail" reached over and took his Cell Phone and then he smashed it against Alex's head. Alex dropped the gun and fell back. "Pony tail" grabbed for the gun and pumped two shots into Alex's chest. Then his car in full throttle squealed off northbound on Route 110. "Russian Bastard" he said as he left.

Jim was at the airport checkout when the announcement came over the loudspeaker. "Will Mr. James Feron, Please call Security As soon as possible. This is an emergency. Mr. Feron please call Security." Jim picked up the Security phone and the Security Chief who was an old retired cop that he knew from the Traffic Division said "Jim, your friend Alex has been shot." " I don't have all the details but he is at Good Samaritan Hospital and is pretty bad shape." Jim stood there for a moment. His plane was ready to leave. He wanted to see Anne, but he had to see how Alex was. What had happened. " He was shot." Who could shoot him, Why? He had to do the right thing and go to the hospital.

When he got to the hospital Alex was in surgery and they told him that he was in very serious condition. Jim sat down in the waiting room and then he gave the nurse his pager number and said "Please call me as soon as there is some word."He drove to the LaGrange Restaurant and sat at the bar and had a "stoly". An old friend was at the bar. Mr. Atchatelli. "Problem" he said. He could see it in Jim's face. "An old friend in Surgery at Good Sam." he said. "They are good over there, I'm on the Board of Directors and I know." "He'll get the best." Have a drink on me." Jim had a "stoly" and another and another. He had more than he usually had. Ray Atchatelli told him "Go home, Jim, this is no good." Jim nodded and paid his bill and went out the door. He got home and fell asleep in his lounge chair .The phone rang and it was Good Sam. Dr. Park." Your friend is out of danger." "He sure is a tough old bird." "Two shots and one hits a rib and is deflected and the other goes through his armpit. Guess the shooter wasn't that good." "Anyway, you can see him tomorrow around 11 o ' clock. "Thanks Doc." said Jim and he went to bed Jim peeked into Alex's room. Alex was awake and spotted him. "Hey comrade, Come on in." "You crazy Russian, what were you trying to do." Alex told him all about the phone call from Jim's nemesis Brian Ferguson. "You should have called the police." "They couldn't have got there on time. Jim." "I had him right in my hands and I let him get away." "I wanted to do this for you, my friend." "Alex did you get a license plate on the truck he was driving?" Alex said "It was 4TU something."

"A red Ford pickup. That's all I got." "That may be enough.""It was a New York plate?" "Yes I remember the Statue of Liberty on the license."

Jim left his friend and went back to the laboratory to check the partial license plate through "Investicom" It took about five minutes for "Investicom" to come up with all the license plates starting with 4TU. It had about fifty plates but only two were on Ford Pickups. One was red. 4TU121 registered to: Brian Smith. 24 Bay Shore Rd. Brightwaters, N.Y. Bright waters was a small hamlet adjacent to Bay Shore with upper middle class residents. He jumped from the computer desk. "Could he have registered the truck with a legitimate address?" He called his friend Steve in the 3rd Precinct and jumped into his car and sped down Route 110 toward the Southern State Parkway. He got off at Udall Road and made a turn into Bay Shore Rd. He approached the house very cautiously although it appeared that no one was home. No cars or truck in the driveway and none nearby . He noticed the door was open and he walked up to it. He was holding his Smith and Wesson behind his hip ready. Steve pulled up and he saw him. "Wait" he yelled. Jim couldn't wait. He was close to his prey. Steve was right behind him as they went in hugging the walls listening for any movement inside. It was a dump with empty beer cans on the floor and an ashtray filled with half smoked Marlboro cigarettes There was a table and on it a note. "Hi there Detective I knew your would get my plate. Sorry I couldn't wait for you and your friends. See ya soon."

As soon as Jim had checked with Alex's doctor and was convinced that he would be alright, he told his friend that he was going back to England. He'd be in close contact but he needed to see Anne. He told him he would check on him daily. Alex said that he would be okay. "I'll have some pretty visiting nurse taking care of me when I get out of here." "Good Luck, in England. Call me with some good news. Bon Voyage."

CHAPTER IX

Hector Thomson stood in front of the receptionist at the Shady Tree Nursing Home in a suburb of Edinburgh, Scotland. He asked to speak to the Director. "Who shall I say is calling?" "Tell him Inspector Thomson from Scotland Yard." and flashed his credentials."I'll get him for you straight away." and she picked up the phone. "Inspector Thomson to see you sir.""He wants you to come to his office. It's down the hall to the right."

Thomson was met outside the Director's office by Dr. Holmes who shook his hand pointed to a chair near his desk. "You're here about Ms. Fulton." "Yes, I want to take her back to Glasgow with me." "I'm afraid she is not ready to leave here." She is still suffering from amnesia and one of our psychiatrists is treating her. He is very hopeful that he can restore her memory. He has been making progress."

"I see" said Thomson. "I am going to stay around town for a day or two. A good friend of hers from the States is coming and he'll be here tomorrow." "I would like to speak to the psychiatrist, if I may?" "How about coming back this afternoon after lunch. Dr. Queen is rather busy. He is the only psychiatrist we have and he won't be able to sit down with you until then." "Okay, I'll come back around two, Will be he be free then?" "Two is good. I"ll arrange that you have his undivided attention then." "Thank you Doctor" said Inspector Thomson and left. Dr. Queen's treatment of Anne Fulton involved some hypnosis. He tried to recreate the events leading up to her fall and injury at the airport. He put her into a trance with the aid of an injection of Sodium Pentothal and slowly he prompted her into the story of how she had an appointment with someone at the airport and had taken a taxi which dropped her off at the entrance. She was reliving the trip in the taxi.

She was out of the cab now and half walking, half running to the departure area. Suddenly she stopped. "You are bumped by a luggage truck and you fall." She went through a series of convulsive moves and he stopped at this point. She came to in a few minutes. She was sweating profusely. "Do you remember anything about the airport?" "Yes, I was seeing off Jim, I can't remember. I was late. I had to hurry. " Dr. Queen had her taken to her room where he had her take a sleeping agent. She went right to sleep. When she woke up in her room, she noticed that the door was open. She stepped out into the hall. There was a nurse's station but the nurse wasn't there. She was in the ladies room. She never dreamed that her absence would cause a problem. Anne walked past the station and toward the elevator. She got on the elevator and took it to the lobby. She calmly walked past the Security Guard and out the door of the nursing home. There was a taxi outside. "Where to, Ma'am?" She said "The London Airport, please, I have to see someone off." The taxi drove out of the driveway and onto a highway. It took them only a half hour to get to the Airport. Anne got out in front of the Airport Entrance. That'll " be two pounds Ma'am" Anne paid no attention and walked past some Red Caps and into the Airport. An Airport Security Agent came up to the taxi.

"You can't park here, you're blocking the entrance." "Hey that woman just beat me on a fare."

"What woman, come on move it or I'll give you a summons." Anne walked aimlessly through the airport until she reached the Information Booth. "Can you tell me the status on Flight 111, British Air?" "You must have the wrong Flight Number. We discontinued that number several months ago." "Where is your flight going?" "To the United States" she said. "There are no flights to the US until much later." "Thank you." said Anne and she walked to the cocktail lounge. It was then that she realized that she had no pocketbook or money. She did have a Pound note stuck wrinkled in her pocket. That would not be enough for a drink, though. She sat down at the bar and asked "How much for a coke?"

"That's one Pound, ma'am." said the bartender. "Give me a coke then, I must have misplaced my purse

"Did I hear you say you lost your purse Ma'am?" asked the bartender. "The Lost and Found is right across the hall." "Thank you I'll try there." Anne finished her coke and walked over to the Lost and Found Desk. "May I help you." a perky young lady asked her. "I lost my purse and I wondered if someone turned it in?" "Let me see we have two purses." "Could this be it." and she held up a small brown pocketbook. "Yes, that's it." "Let me see, it's empty. I'm supposed to get some ID from you, but since there's no valuables in it, I guess I can let you have it." and handed over the purse to Anne. Anne waited until she was far enough away from the desk until she looked inside. It was empty just as the clerk said. But wait there was a little pocket on the inside which was not very noticeable. She felt inside the pocket. There was an American Express Card inside.

The name was Ann Martin and it had not yet expired. She knew that she could not use it because she did not know the pin so she just stuck it back in the bag.

Anne hadn't eaten for several hours now and she was a little weak from hunger. She sat down on a bench and saw a small bag of potato chips. She reached over and opened it. It had only a few crumbs, but she ate them. She suddenly saw spots and heard this pounding in her ears. She passed out on the bench.

The EMT put some smelling salts under her nose and she woke up.

"Alright Miss?" "I think we should take you to Emergency and have you checked out." She didn't argue and they put her on a Gurney and took her away in the ambulance.

Jim Feron was busy picking up his luggage when the ambulance left. He looked outside when he heard the sound of the siren. He continued to wait at the carousel for his bags.

"Ann Martin" was checked into the hospital and put in a room and given a intravenous. A clerk came in the room and started paper work on her. "Name?" "Ann"she said "Oh yes Ms. Martin" "We have your personal effects with your American Express card." "What's your date of birth?" "I don't know." "Where do you live?" "I don't know." "Who can we contact in your family?" "I don't know." Frustrated . The clerk went out and spoke to a nurse. The nurse would notify one of the doctors.

The staff at the"Shady Rest Home" were in a panic. One of the patients could not be accounted for. Dr. Holmes had the station nurse in his office. "This is irresponsible." "You are terminated as of this minute." "The whole reputation of this hospital is at stake because of your laxity." Dr. Holmes was on the phone with members of his staff. "I want a complete search of the premises." His intercom buzzed. "Mr. Thomson is here." said the voice. "Send him right in." Dr. Holmes embarrassingly told Thomson of Anne's disappearance. While they sat in his office Holmes received a call that all of the rooms, closets and spaces in the building were searched. The grounds were searched but to no avail. She was gone. Thomson sat there and ventured a suggestion. "Do you have taxis outside?" "Yes, we do." said Holmes. "Are they always the same taxi company?" "No sometimes they bring people here to visit and those taxis can come from anywhere in the city." Thomson left with this possible clue. He would check all of the taxi companies to see if any of them picked up a female from the home.

It was his unpleasant duty to inform Jim of Anne's new disappearance. "Jim, I won't rest until I find her for you." "How long can you stay?" This was Friday and Jim said he would stay over the weekend. He tried to help Hector in his search of a taxi that had picked up a fare at the "Shady Rest Home" on Friday. They called taxi company after taxi company. "Listen, it's getting toward supper time. "I'm gonna make a few more calls and then I'll meet you for cocktails and supper in about an hour. You go to your hotel and get cleaned up and I'll meet you in the lobby in two hours." Jim left for the Royal British Hotel. There was a nice bar in the hotel called the "Glendale Room" He would meet Hector there.

He had just started on his first "story" when Hector came in. He was excited. He had found a taxi company "Imperial Taxi Company" and one of their drivers had picked up a young woman at the Shady Rest Home. He took her to the airport. "I've got a call into the airport security and after we eat we'll drive over and see the Chief of Security. Jim couldn't wait until after they ate. He insisted on going now.

CHAPTER X

The Airport Security Chief looked over his incident log and found that a woman had been transported to the hospital apparently semi conscious. Her name was Ann Martin. The only identification on her was an American Express card. Her description matched Anne Fulton. Hector and Jim drove to the hospital where Anne had been taken. She was in a semi private room and they had a chat with the station nurse before they visited the room."She is suffering from sort of amnesia." "Physically she is fine. We are taking the IV off of her. She's had her dinner and we were waiting for the hospital security to check out the American Express Card. "Don't bother." said Hector." "We know who is really is." Her name is Anne Fulton and she is a missing patient from the "Shady Rest Home" As soon as she can travel I will be making arrangements for her to go back. She was undergoing psychiatric treatment there." Jim couldn't wait to see her but he was to be disappointed. She looked at him as he entered the room. A blank stare on her face. She didn't know him. He tried to hold a conversation with her. "Anne, it's me Jim Feron, remember we met at St. Andrews?" "I'm sorry, sir, I just don't seem to recall you." she said and then drifted off to sleep. The next day Anne was taken back to "Shady Rest". She would resume her treatment. Jim left two days later. He would keep in touch with Dr. Holmes. The trip back was long or so it seemed. He read a copy of the N.Y. Times before taking a nap There was an interesting story in the Times about the Assassination of John F. Kennedy. The tape made at the scene which had caused a stir during the Assassinations Committee Investigation was being made public. Anyone who wanted to hear the roar of the motorcycles and then the shots that were fired could obtain a copy. "How ghoulish" he thought. And then he went off to sleep.

Alex was in the laboratory working. His arm in a sling. "Hey Comrade, How are you." He knew all about Anne's adventure and Jim's disappointing meeting in the hospital. He never mentioned it. He was excited about a new development with "Investicom" I think we have our sound identification program perfected." "We have the perfect vehicle to try it." "You'll have to use your connections, though." "Did you read about the recent kidnapping of Mary Grey?" There has been a follow up to it. A phone call from the kidnapper. He wants 1 Million Dollars from the family." "They own a controlling share in a major TV station." "I want you to see if you can get a copy of the kidnappers telephone call." Jim called an old friend in the Major Case Squad. They were working in conjunction with the FBI. "Lt. Kennedy, How the hell are you, Jim Feron.'"Jimmy, old pal, where're you been. I miss our drinking nights at Forlini's Restaurant on Baxter Street." "I went back to school and I'm working with a professor from MIT. We are involved in a computer project." "Really, Oh now I remember, one of the guys here mentioned that you and some Lexmendo or whatever just got a grant from Uncle Sam. How's it going"Fred, this thing may revolutionize law enforcement. Some of it's programs already are having an influence." "We want to try an experiment that may turn out to be fruitful in your recent kidnapping. "We 'd like to get a copy of the tape of the phone call from the kidnapper." "Oh Jim, I don't know. The FBI is the lead agency on this case and you know how they are. I don't think they will give it to you.""I'll tell you what though, I'll try. It's really tough because it's an ongoing investigation and a lot of pressure is being put on us. It's been three days and we had two calls from this guy. He wants1 Mil and he has been giving us complicated messages as to how he wants it delivered. He has a scheme which I can't talk about that is really elaborate. And the money, he wants it in small bills. Can you imagine 1 Million in small bills." "Let me get back to you."

A couple of hours later, Lt. Fred Kennedy called Jim at the laboratory."Hey you guys must know somebody. They gave me both of the tapes and told me to deliver them to you. "I'll pick them up" said Jim No one was allowed inside the lab besides Alex and himself.

Alex inserted the mini-tape into the cassette, which had a cable running to the computer. He turned on the program and then they listened to the tape.

The first tape was about three minutes long. The second ran for almost ten minutes with the kidnappers elaborate scheme for the delivery of the ransom. "Investicom" was humming, analyzing the tapes. The program took a half an hour and then the printer started to click on and out came the data on the tapes.

The first tape identified a sound in the background as a train, but not just any train. It identified it as an electric from the Long Island Rail Road. The second tape was very interesting. It heard a truck in the background and then it continued to search for an identification of the kind of truck.

It came up with a make of truck Then it went into it's database as to delivery trucks that used that make of truck.

UPS, FedEx, Airborne Express until and the most amazing find of the search. It identified the truck as a Fed Ex truck. The identification showed that the Fed Ex truck had been sitting with the motor running for two minutes. This meant that it was making a delivery. Jim called Fred and asked him to find out through Fed Ex Security where one of their trucks made a delivery at 2:30 PM on Monday. Fred called Fed Ex.

Fred called Jim with the information. Fed Ex had made a delivery at 2:30 PM on Monday to a home on Suffolk Avenue in Brentwood, Long Island. There were several homes across from the Long Island Rail Road station. Surveillance was set up immediately in the vicinity in the Station Master's office. There were three houses that were suspect. The house that the Fed Ex truck stopped at and the one's on either side of it. The house on the left looked very normal. The house on the right had two pickups and a motorcycle in the driveway and looked like no one had ever mowed the lawn. Maybe. The house in the middle, where the Fed Ex truck was parked was very quiet with cars in the driveway. It looked like no one was home. The FBI got wiretaps for all three houses. The judge gave them a lot of leeway in granting the orders. The wiretaps proved fruitful.

The house with the pickups and the motorcycle was the one. It was an old style house, a one family with an upstairs window, and a porch. A man in his thirties wearing a vest with a Skull and Crossbones on it and the name"Blue Angels." came out and drove his motorcycle to a local supermarket and went in and bought groceries. The phone calls had not com from the home, but conversation from the house to other locations indicated strongly that these were the kidnappers.

It now up to the professionals to decide when and how to raid the house. Mary Grey's safety was paramount. If she was still alive. They had to assume that she was. In the back of the house there were some oak trees and they were rather close to the electrical wires. Detectives disguised as workers from the Electric Company pulled up. They had electric chain saws for cutting down trees. One knocked on the door and informed a man, dressed in a leather jacket with "Blue Angels" on it, that they would be working in his back yard. They had to cut down a tree. It would take about a half an hour, The man reluctantly agreed. They started working in the back yard. They were watched from an upstairs window. From the telephone conversations it was determined that there were at least three men inside the house.

They had to figure out another ruse to get in the front. A large delivery truck pulled up in front of the house. The delivery men opened the tail gate and proceeded to take out a large crate which read "Refrigerator". They were watched from a front window. The two delivery men went up to the door. The same man came to the door and inquired "What are you doing here?"

"Delivery of a refrigerator." "You must have the wrong address. No one here ordered a refrigerator." "Is this your name and address?" said one of the delivery men and the man stepped out on the porch to look at the delivery slip. One of the delivery men (Detectives) pulled him aside out of view of the window. They anesthetized him with a hypodermic. The result was so quick that he was unable to make a sound. A second man came to the door.

"Hey Joe who are these guys, what's the story." He too was taken down very quietly and quickly. Now they were dragging the crate inside the house. The man who had been watching upstairs came down to see what was going on.

Meanwhile the tree cutters in the back seeing that their observer had left the window entered the back door. The third man was taken easily and all of the Detectives were now inside of the house. They searched very cautiously upstairs and into the basement It didn't take long to find little Mary Grey in an upstairs bed room, with her hands tied and a piece of tape over her mouth. She was unhurt .

Again it became Jim's job to make sure that the work of "Investicom" was not compromised by the news media. The only ones who were aware of "Investicoms" search for the truck were Lt. Kennedy and his FBI counterpart in Major Case Kidnapping Task Force. They were wise enough not to disclose any information. Lt. Kennedy had a meeting with the Police Commissioner and the FBI's Special Agent in Charge of the New York Office had to be told and so the information was not leaked out about the "fantastic" find made through sound identification.

CHAPTER XI

Jim went through his luggage that he had thrown in a corner of the closet. The luggage he used from his trip to England. Inside he had the usual copy of a magazine that they put in the flap in front of your seat with all the ads and things you can buy that are not usually advertised any where else like Air Conditioner units and DVD players that record and electronic stuff such as that. It had the usual crossword puzzle. He had done half of it. He had a city map of London and some business cards "Dr. Holmes, Director. Shady Rest Nursing Home." He put them aside.

He had the copy of the New York Times that he had been reading on the trip. He was about to throw it in the trash can when the article about the tape of JFK's assassination caught his eye. His mind started to work. He took the paper and brought it to the laboratory.

There was Alex in ahead of him as usual. "Half day?" he kidded. It was only 8 o'clock in the morning. Jim put down a bag with two containers of coffee and a couple of bagels. A salt one for him and a Sesame one for Alex. "Too much butter on this." said Alex and he took a plastic knife and removed a big wad of butter.

"Alex, I have a project for "Investicom" "It may be the biggest thing we've ever tried with it." "And we don't have to tell anyone what

we are doing." "All the information we need is more or less public."
"Sounds interesting, What are we talking about." "The Assassination
of the President of the United States." said Jim. Alex's eyes lit up as
Jim handed him the N.Y. Times with the page containing the article
about the tape. "The sound database." His mind raced. He and Jim
were definitely on the same page as far as what they wanted to try.

They were going to get the tape and play it through "Investicom"
and see what foreign sounds it could pick up. There was a report
of a fourth shot. This was disclosed in the Assassination Hearings
Investigation. A fourth shot fired by whom. Not Oswald, but perhaps
a second man in Conspiracy to kill the President.

The tape was made available through a mail order house. They
faxed a request for the tape and paid for it with their business credit
card. It would take several days for delivery. They waited patiently,
meanwhile still working and improving "Investicom"

The tape that they got from the mail order house was not what
they expected. It was a poor copy of a lot police transmissions and
News Media and it had the sound of a couple of shots that could be
heard while the News Commentator was describing the Presidents
motorcade past the Texas Book Depository. What they had wanted
was the transmission made of the Dallas Police Department. One of
their motorcycle officers had inadvertently left his microphone open
and it was broadcasting over the Dallas Police Radio network. Jim
called up an old friend who had worked in the New York County
District Attorney's Office. This Detective had gone to work for
the Select House Committee on Assassinations. Retired Detective
Joe Bastri. Joe told Jim that he still kept in touch with some of the
Investigators and he thought that one of them had kept a copy of the
tape that he was interested in. "Why do you want it?" "You haven't
become a collector have you?" "No" said Jim and he told Joe about his

computer project and that they wanted to conduct an experiment with the tape. Joe would call him back after he made some inquiries.

A few days passed and then Jim got a call from Bastri. "I got the tape for you and it's a very good copy. A three to one." A one to one would have been great, but a three to one was pretty good. "I'm sending it to you by Fed Ex Priority.

You'll have it tomorrow." "Thanks a lot Joe and what are you dong with your self these days anyway?" "Nothing, Jimbo, After the House Committee job I thought my resume would open a lot of doors but it didn't. I got a job with the State Insurance Fund investigating Workman's Compensation Cases." "After a few years there I retired completely. I play a pretty good game of golf. I"ll take you on some day if you want" "Be glad to Joe, but you'll have to give me some strokes." "The tape came as promised and the two researchers went to work putting the into "Investicom" It took some time for "Investicom" to study the data coming out of the tape. The tape did not have what you would call "four shots". There were three distinctive shots heard on the tape, but a Dallas Police recording contained four impulses are the results of the sound of four gunshots that were fired in Dealey Plaza. One of the impulses was caused by a shot that came from the grassy knoll. The Conclusions and Research of the House Select Committee on Assassinations had concluded in their report that there was a fourth shot and it came from a shooter placed at the grassy knoll.

"Investicom" would verify that there were in fact four shots fired at the President of the United States. It would come up with information that was not discovered as a result of the House Select Committee's Investigation."Investicom" buzzed and clicked for several hours searching it's sound database. The same database that had solved the Mary Grey kidnapping. This, however was the case of the Century. The murder of the President of the United States. John F. Kennedy. Many books had been written with theories of a conspiracy. In 1975 a Committee was established to investigate the Assassination.

Jim and Alex waited patiently for the results of the search. It took almost eight hours. The results spewed out on the printer. It reminded Jim of the teletype machines that they had in the NYPD police precincts that told of Stolen Cars, Robberies, Homicides, Missing Persons, Descriptions of perpetrators, Promotions, Parades and so on.

The information was this: "Investicom" verified that there were in fact four shots fired. It gave the locations of the shots. Three from the area of the Texas Book Depository. One from the areas of "the grassy knoll"And then it identified the make, model of the firearm used. Three shots fired by a C2766, a MANNLICHER CARCANO Rifle. This is the rifle that was recovered at the Texas Book Depository. The fourth shot was fired by a C2766 MANNLICHER CARCANO Rifle. The same as used by Oswald. This meant that the shooter from "the grassy knoll" had used the same kind of rifle as Oswald. "Why not?" said Jim. "It makes sense." "The only bullets they found were from a MANNLICHER."

Now could "Investicom" go further in the investigation? Jim went into the and found the following information: The rifle found on the sixth floor of the Texas Book Depository was a 6.5 Millimeter Mannlicher Carcano model 91/38 made in Italy between 1939 and 1940. The rifle found was 40.2 inches long and the weight of it was eight pounds. Attached to it was a four power telescope sight made in Japan.

The Depository rifle could not fire two shots in less than 2.3 seconds. The Warren Commission established that between the first and the last shot there were no more than seven seconds, so that only one bullet could have caused Kennedy and Governor Connolly's wounds. When the FBI tried to re-enact the assassination with the same rifle, not one of their expert shooters could repeat Oswald's performance, considering the characteristics of the rifle. There was some speculation as to who bought the rifle at the Klein's Sports Goods Company. All of the experts did not agree that it was Oswald's signature on the order. This made for more mystery about the assassination.

"Now what about the second rifle" thought Jim. There had been various disparaging remarks made about the Mannlicher which had tainted it's reputation. The most damaging was a story about a W W II Allied Soldier who was killed firing a Mannlicher. Allegedly the firing pin ruptured the primer causing the gases to propel the firing pin backward d into the face of the shooter. No one knew the name of the alleged soldier or the circumstances or any other probable facts of this incident. It had also been reported that Mussolini knocked the Mannlicher as part of his for the performance of the Italian army. Some believed that the Mannlilcher displayed a greater accuracy than the M1Garand rifle used by the US Army. It was also interesting to note that the Italian Army NATO rifle team used the M91 rifle in matches and came out in the top positions.

All of this information only proved that the rifle was a competent weapon and there were an awful lot of them out there. How could anyone find the second Mannlicher? At least there was evidence showing where Oswald had allegedly purchased the rifle. The second rifle would never be recovered so tracing it was impossible. It was at this point that Jim and Alex terminated their research of the Assassination. They did however pass along the information to Congress since they felt obligated because of the grant awarded to them by the government. This would prove to create a problem.

CHAPTER XII

The House Select Committee on Science and Technology had started their hearings. They were looking closely at some grants that were awarded and the grant received by Jim and Alex for "Investicom" was one of them. Both Jim and Alex received subpoenas to appear at one of their hearings.

"Tell us a little about your project Mr. Feron.: Congresswoman Hilton asked. "Well it deals mostly with locating people. It has data bases that can help to find fugitives and missing persons. "Give the Committee a detail ed list of all the programs that are stored in your"Investicom". "I'm afraid I can't do that,Congresswoman Hilton." said Jim frowning. "What do you mean, sir. You can't give a list?" "No Ma'am, some of the programs are considered sensitive and Top Secret.

"Do you or your partner, Mr. Lermindov have a clearance." "No we don't, it's just that-----" And she cut him off with "Then how can you claim that the programs are Top" Secret." "Well they're not Top Secret in the sense that there are government cleared. Just that to compromise the programs would do a lot of harm to the value of the computer."

The interrogation went on and on with the Congresswoman becoming more and more annoyed at Jim's responses. She was not getting the information she wanted. Finally she pointed her finger at Jim. "Mr. Feron, you received a government grant of $250,000 and you are not going to supply this Committee with information about your computer.""

The Committee interrogated Lermindov and Congresswoman Hilton received the same responses. Alex and Jim were not about to reveal all the programs hidden inside "Investicom"

Members of the Major Case Squad, Fred Kennedy and FBI were interrogated. They disclosed how 'Investicom" was instrumental in solving the "Mary Grey" kidnapping. There was no doubt that this computer was useful to law enforcement. If Jim or Alex had their way, even this much about "Investicom" would not be disclosed,They could see the headlines the next day.

"Retired Detective and MIT Professor refuse to disclose programs stored in their Super Computer"They were happy to receive a grant from the United States Government, however, they will not cooperate with the House Committee on Science and Technology." This is exactly how the article read.

After a closed session of the Committee where some of the more reasonable members prevailed. It was ruled that Jim and Alex could keep the grant, however, they would have to undergo a comprehensive background investigation to determine their suitability to hold a "Top Secret" and above clearance. "Investicoms" data was to be ruled above Top Secret and only a handful of persons would be able to access it's data and only through Jim and Alex after they passed their investigation.

Alex and Jim knew that the background would take at least six weeks to complete and during that time "Investicom" would stand down. They filled out all the necessary forms about their Personal Histories, a Personal Security Questionnaire. Jim knew that the background investigation would take about six weeks so he decided that this would be a good time to go back to England and see Anne. Alex was going to go with him but he would stay south while Jim went up to the "Shady Rest Nursing Home".

CHAPTER XIII

Before Jim went to the Shady Rest he called on Hector Thomson. Hector greeted him warmly. "Say I was reading something about you and your computer in the "London Times" the other day. Gave you a bit of a hard time did they? "Bureaucrats, they're all the same, no matter what country." "Going up to see Anne, eh?" "I check with them up there every week. She is regaining some of her memory but it is slow."

"Maybe seeing you will shock some of it back. Good Luck." "Have time for a pint this evening before you go?" "No thanks" said Jim. "When I come back we'll bend the elbows a little, I promise."

After consulting with Dr. Holmes. Jim was allowed to visit Anne in her room. She greeted him with a smile after he introduced himself. "Did I know you?" she said. "Yes, we only met a couple of times but we became good friends." "Are you allowed to leave the home to go out to dinner?" "Yes, it just has to be cleared through Dr. Holmes." Dr. Holmes actually recommended that Jim take Anne out for the day. Since they were not that far from St. Andrews, he took her to the hotel restaurant where they first met. He was hoping that the familiar surrounding might help her. Several times during the meal she stopped and looked very pensive. He thought he saw some recognition in her eyes several times but then it disappeared. They had a nice lunch and then went downtown past the golf course and down the main street with all the shops. He took her into one shop and bought her a windbreaker with the logo"St. Andrews Golf Course" on it. As they left the shop she took his hand and then they walked back to the car hand in hand. He was falling in love all over again with her.

He was allowed to take her out several more times. It was a courtship. He took her to a movie and they saw "Love Story" with Ali McGraw. On another occasion they just sat in the recreation room, which had a nice sofa and they watched television together. This one night they were watching an old Bing Crosby movie and the feature song in the movie was "The Second Time Around" As Bing sang "Love is lovelier the second time around" he looked into her eyes and kissed her. It was a tender kiss. Where they were was not exactly the place for heavy necking. He took her back to her room and kissed her again. "Goodnight" he said and then he told her that he would have to be going back to the United States again. She looked sad but he told her he would call her every day and as soon as she was able to leave the home he would come back and take her back home. They would have one more day together and then he told her as he was about to leave."Anne, I know you don't remember me, but that's all right. Maybe someday you will, anyway I love you and I want to marry you." She smiled "I can't answer you now, but as soon as Dr. Holmes tells me I'm able to be released from here, I'll give you my answer."

Jim checked in with Hector Thomson as he said he would. Alex had spent most of his time at the British Computer Society. He received a Distinguished Fellowship Award. Jim remarked "You old coot, why didn't you tell me you were getting an award?" "Ah, shucks,

Jim" said Alex with a Russian accented cowboy drawl. "I didn't want to spoil your visit with Anne." Both of them decided they would celebrate with a pint or two with Hector.

Hector's office was in turmoil. Detective Inspector's running around. Telephones ringing incessantly and Hector in his office with several Inspectors frantic about something, obviously a serious situation. It didn't take much for Jim and Alex to recognize that there was some sort of crisis and from the looks of the faces, a very serious one.

Hector came out of his office as soon as he saw Jim. "Jim, I'm afraid we can't go for that drink. Something has come up." "That's too bad, Hector, Anything we can do, I mean can you meet us a little later on. We'll probably be still in the bar until late." "Jim, I've got my hands full right now. As soon as things quiet down, I'll try to make it for a drink. See you later."

Jim and Alex had just about given up on Hector. Jim was on his fourth "Stoly". One over his usual limit and Alex was having a Grand Marnier "100" when Hector came into the bar. "What a day?" " I've been going since 8 this morning. " "Can you talk about it?" said Jim.

"I guess I can tell you, it'll probably make the papers anyway. You can't keep anything quiet these days." "One of our MP's (Member of Parliament) is missing. He just so happens that he is on some super secret Intelligence Committee and some papers may be missing also." "I don't want to be a smart ass. Hector, but have you checked his phone records for the past 48 hours."

"Could be he has a girl friend, You know something innocent." "Jim, I don't think we have done anything like that." "Wait here."Hector went to the phone and made a call then returned to the bar. "It'll be done. We should get the info by the time we have another drink." "I'll just nurse this one." said Jim. "Ah come on."said Alex."Alright, give me a Drambuie and I'll nurse that one."

After an hour and two Drambuies, the call came in for Hector. Jim and Alex watched his reaction as he received the information on the telephone records. "Jim, I think we've got something. He's made several calls to a place in Blackpool. There was a villa near the beach. Hector asked Jim and Alex to drive to Blackpool with him. His people would meet them there.

It took them a little over four hours to drive there. Hector drove and Jim and Alex dozed and dreampt about Anne and St. Andrews. It was dark when they got to Blackpool.

The address was to a large house with a big piece of property, that was enclosed with a brick fence and an iron gate. The house had a light on downstairs. It had a circular driveway, but they were unable to see if any vehicles were in the driveway. Hector had contacted the rest of his squad, who were stuck in a traffic jam because of an accident.

They would not be able to get there for at least an hour. Hector was impatient. He gave Jim an extra pistol, a Luger that he had. Alex would stay in the car and operate the radio to direct the squad when they got close. Hector's plan was to climb over the fence and approach the house in the dark and try to see what if anything was going on inside.

Both Hector and Jim scaled the fence rather easily but they were to encounter something they hadn't planned on. Dogs. Two Dobermans came racing towards them, barking and snarling. They cornered Jim and Hector. Hector went down with the one dog on top of him and so did Jim. They were strong dogs and Jim could feel the hot breath of the dog on top of him on his face. He raised his elbow and the dog locked his jaws on it. His arm burned with the pain. With his other hand he reached into his pocket and withdrew a knife. He buried it in the dogs stomach. The dog squealed and went limp .He was up in a flash to help Hector who had his own problem with the other dog. Jim jumped on the dog's back and he buried his knife into the dog. He had killed both dogs in less than a minute.

Did the noise from the encounter give them away? They didn't know. They crept slowly toward the house. Apparently the people inside hadn't heard the commotion. They were now able to look inside the window. Inside was a man in a chair tied up with duct tape. A man was standing over him and he had a hypodermic needle that he was about to insert in the man's arm. The man in the chair was the Member of Parliament. They couldn't wait any longer so they climbed through the window and attacked the man with the needle. He was not alone. Before they knew it they were in a battle with two men and a woman. It became a pitch battle and neither Jim or Hector were able to use their weapons. Chairs went over and tables and lamps shattered.

Outside Alex waited with the radio. The squad had broken through the traffic jam and was only minutes away. The skirmish inside the house continued with no apparent winners or losers Finally Hector broke free from one of the men and pulled out his gun. He fired two shots into the air and his assailant froze. Then he pointed the gun at Jim's opponent and he froze too. The woman ran toward the door. The woman was apprehended at the gate by Hector's squad, who had just arrived. The MP was released, but he had been drugged. The MP had been seeing this woman on the sly. She lured him to the house in Blackpool. He went there immediately after leaving his office and had some innocent papers with him. The two men and the woman had hoped to try to get him to disclose the whereabouts of some important documents. They were agents of

Sadam. Hussein Hector couldn't thank Jim enough for his hunch about the phone records. "I don't know why I didn't think of that myself?. He said. "I guess it was the excitement." "Hector, I am just happy that Alex and I were able to help you. Please don't mention our involvement in this when you talk to the press." "Okay, Jim, I think I understand." "Are you two leaving to go back to the States?" "Yes tomorrow." "I'll keep in touch and I will be back soon." "I know you will." said Hector. He shook Jim's hand vigorously and patted Alex on the back.

They were on the plane early the next day and arrived at JFK in the afternoon. Jim had a melancholy feeling as they drove from the airport. He wished he could still be with Anne.

There were several messages on their answering machine when they got back. One was from the FBI. Their Security Clearances had been granted. Another was from the House Committee and it too had good news. The House's investigation into grants was completed and they would keep their grant. They would have to set up a system whereby they had a liaison with the Bureau for the use of

"Investicom" as a law enforcement tool. Their contact with the FBI was to be with Special Agent Harmon. He would be calling on them for a meeting soon to set up procedures.

The meeting was held at 26 Federal Plaza and lasted a week. But when they were finished several steps were put in place as to how "Investicom" would be used. Unfortunately, there would be no more individual "contracts" such as the one with Vito D'Angelo. Any law enforcement requests for assistance would have to be cleared by the FBI. This presented a problem at first. Jim and Alex were allowed to use their own judgment as to the use of the computer, when time became a factor. they would still have to inform Harmon as soon as they could.

After the clearance was granted and the procedures with the FBI put into place everything started to run fairly smooth. There were the usual bureaucratic glitches with the Bureau but"Investicom" was earning it's federal grant

CHAPTER IV

It was sometime after this that Jim received a call from a liaison officer from the White House. His name was William Colin and he informed Jim that he was wanted for a special conference at the White House, This was to be "Top Secret". Alex would stay and operate 'Investicon" A plane would be dispatched for him at Republic Airport, in Farmingdale, N.Y., which was very close to the warehouse that they used. Jim was to come alone. The plane arrived in the afternoon and Jim boarded and was whisked down to Washington. The flight was short and when they landed a limousine was on hand to take them directly to the White House. 'Gee" Jim thought "Am I going to meet the president?" Jim did not meet the President but he met one of his top advisors. William Colin. Colin was a tall man about 6 feet three, trim and had a shock of white hair. He had piercing blue eyes and he looked very serious. He had Jim sit down at a conference table with two Generals and and an Admiral. "Now let's get down to business." "Mr. Feron, this is General Wade, United States Army, General Stock, United States Marine Corps and Admiral Pine, United States Navy. " Jim stood up and shook hands with the military. They also rose to greet him. "It's an honor." he said.

"And for us too" one of them said. "We've heard a lot about "Investicom" "And now maybe she will perform a great service to it's country." said Colin, talking about it as if it were a human being. There were folders in front of each of them with their respective names on them. Jim was anxious to open his but he didn't dare until instructed. Colin didn't waste any time telling him what the project was." Mr. Feron, you and your computer are going to help us find Bin Laden.""We are using every resource available to locate and apprehend this criminal." Jim's face flushed. His desire to help find the World's number one fugitive was overwhelming. He had a determined look on his face. Colin looked at him and knew that he had chosen the right man to join this committee.

Now they would open the folders. Inside was the usual profile of Bin Laden and then there were several documents with the stamp "Top Secret" on them. Colin asked everyone to please take a few minutes to go over the folders. There was a pot of coffee on the table and each of them filled a cup for themselves. They read slowly while they sipped their coffees.

Jim read slowly. Here was a profile on the Most Wanted Man in the world. There were Intelligence reports intermingled with information from the Media. Jim looked up a couple of times as if he was taking a test, sneaking a peek at the Generals. They too were engrossed in reading the reports.

Jim read that Osama was born in 1955 and that his father ran a very lucrative construction business. He was a Yemeni. Bin Laden's mother was Syrian and Bin Laden was her only son. He had tutors and nannies and was pretty much pampered. When he was only thirteen, his father was killed in a helicopter crash and he inherited 80 million dollars. When he was nineteen he attended the university of King Abdul Aziz and he received a degree in civil engineering.

He attended some of Beiruts flashiest nightclubs and was known to be a heavy drinker, brawler and womanizer.

Three events seemed to influence Bin Laden. They were the Peace Treaty signed by Egypt and Israel, then the invasion of Afghanistan by the Soviets and the Iranian Revolution that toppled the Shah.

Bin Laden allegedly went to Afghanistan during the invasion. During the first years of the war he traveled throughout Saudi Arabia raising money. Some of the money came from the Saudi Government, some from official Mosques, some from the kingdom's financial and business elite including his father's construction business, "The Bin Laden Group".

Later in 1984, Bin Laden operated out of a border town called Peshawar, in Pakistan. It was a staging area for the war. He visited hospitals where wounded Arab and Afghan soldiers had been brought. He was called the "Saudi Prince"

He was dressed elegantly. He had on a knee length tunic top and wore tailored English trousers. He wore custom made Beal Brothers boots. He went from bed to bed distributing chocolates and nuts and carefully taking each man's name and address. Later the man's family would receive a generous check.

More stories told of an enigmatic Saudi who arrived in an unmarked Military Transport plane which landed in the ungovernable tribal areas of the Pakistan- Afghan border. He brought in bulldozers and heavy construction equipment. They were used to build tunnels and storage depots. The man was Bin Laden and the equipment was supplied by the Bin Laden Group

When Jim and the Generals had finished reading the reports, William Colin asked them to take a few minutes to engage in an informal discussion. One of the Generals started with an outline of the search for Bin Laden and current aspects of the search. Several bombing raids had been conducted in areas that were suspected of being his headquarters in the desert. So far no evidence had been obtained that he had been killed, however there was a report that he had received a shrapnel wound in one arm. Jim asked "How many video tapes of Bin Laden do we have currently?" The Admiral responded "I am the Chief Intelligence Officer for the Joint Chiefs and I can tell you that we have some twenty-five tapes but the most current that number about five."

" I would like copies of those tapes." said Jim. "I have an idea to run them through our computer "Investicom" "I want to study the backgrounds of the tapes"

"The computer may be capable of identifying certain locations where the tapes were made."

The Military people's eyes widened. "You mean to tell us that you have that capability?" "Yes, we have tried it on a small scale and now is the time to really put it to the test."

"Mr. Feron, I'm really impressed." said the Admiral and the Generals nodded. "You know my Grandfather was a Captain in the New York City Police Department. It was when Jimmy Walker was the Mayor." "He left because the department was so corrupt in those days. He couldn't stand it anymore." "I have a fondness for the NY cops though." "When I came into the city I was assigned a Detective from the Bureau of Special Services and they treated me royally." "How long are you retired Jim?" "It'll be seventeen years." said Jim. "That's a while to be away from the "job", anyway, we are all happy that you and your computer could be part of this mission and when we break for the day, we would like you to join us for dinner and cocktails in the Officers Club this evening." Jim agreed but he pressed on obtaining the tapes so that he could get "Investicom" to work as soon as possible. The Admiral told him that he would have the tapes for him this evening.

Jim had a pleasant dinner with the Generals and as he bid them all good night, a Marine Sergeant handed him a brief case which contained the tapes. He slept well that night in a room setup for him in the White House. He asked about the President, who was away in Camp David. Colin said that the President was briefed on the details of their meeting. Just before he retired the phone rang in his bed room suite. He recognized the voice immediately. It was the President of the United States. "Mr. Feron, I am so sorry I did not get to meet you, but Colin has kept me up to date and I just wanted to welcome you to this important mission. I look forward to meeting you the next time you come to Washington. Until then, God Speed with your, I mean our work." There was no mistaking who it was and Jim simply said "Thank you sir and God Bless you and God Bless America."

CHAPTER XV

Jim could hardly wait for the plane to land so he could get back to the laboratory. Alex was sitting there waiting for him. He had the programs all prepared for the tape analysis. The tape analysis consisted of determining from the background of Osama's videos, and where he was in Afghanistan at the time of the video taping. There were several mountain ranges that appeared in the background along with other indicators such as rock formations and the color of the desert terrain. All of these pieces of evidence would be analyzed by "Investicom" and then hopefully, the computer would determine where Bin Laden was in Afghanistan, if it was Afghanistan or perhaps Pakistan.

The tapes were inserted into a VCR which connected to the computer and it analyzed them frame by frame. This would take a long time. It was expected that the analysis would take at least a week. The computer would run day and night, clicking and ticking making whizzing sounds, lights flashing while it went to work on the tapes.

Alex said "Jim, there is no need for both of us to stay here babysitting "Investicom"

"Why don't you take the week off and do something, anything. I'll keep in touch and in a week's time come back and we'll both wait out the final hours of the analysis.

Okay ?"

Jim longed to return to Scotland and to the Shady Rest Home, but before he make the trip again, he called Dr. Holmes. Dr. Holmes told him that Anne was progressing so well that they may have to release her. She had progressed to the point that she could decide herself whether or not to stay for more treatment or see her own doctor. Holmes pointed out that she would possibly never completely regain all of her memory. "Can I talk to her on the phone?" said Jim anxiously.

"Yes , of course, she's in town right now shopping, but when she comes back I'll have her call you." "Thanks, Doc." and Jim held the phone away from his ear for a moment, reflecting and then put it down.

Anne did call after about an hour. "Jim, I feel so much better, I want to leave and go home.""Anne, I'd like you to come to the United States." "I'll pay your fare, you could leave tomorrow and I'd meet you at the airport." "How about it?" She paused in the conversation for a minute and then said "I'd love to, I'll start packing tonight." "You don't have to pay for me though, I'll get the tickets and call you just before I leave." Jim was so excited. He said "Goodbye, honey, I love you." and then she said something that kind of worried him. She said "I love you too, no matter what happens."

Her plane would arrive on Monday, the day after he called. He waited in the laboratory with Alex until it was time to leave and meet her at the airport. He left about three hours before her plane was scheduled to land at JFK. It was a smooth ride with very little traffic. He reached the Van Wyck Expressway which led to the entrance to the Airport. It was then that his cell phone went off. He pulled into the driveway of the International Hotel and parked. He was very early and he was curious about the call. It was Alex. "What's up, Comrade." Alex sounded very somber.

"Jim, come on back, she's not on the plane." What do you mean she's not on the plane?" "Come on back, Jim, I'll tell you all about it when you get back."Jim kept asking him "What happened?" but Alex just kept saying

"Come on back, it's important that you come back now." Jim didn't question any further. He turned the car around and drove back as fast as he could. He was going between 75 and 80 when he saw the police car in his rear view mirror. He pulled over and when the officer approached he identified himself as a retired Detective.

"What's the hurry, Mac?" said the cop. "I got an emergency, otherwise I wouldn't do this to you." he said. The cop saw that he had a serious problem and he let him go. "Hey. Take it slow, I don't want to see you up ahead wrapped around some tree.

"Thanks, buddy, I'll be as careful as I can." said Jim and he sped off. Jim pulled up in the driveway of the laboratory. He could see Alex looking out of the window anxiously waiting for him. "Alex, please tell me what's up with Anne?" Alex looked at him and tears ran down his cheeks. "She's , Jim." "An automobile accident." "She was in a taxi heading for the Airport when the cab collided with a gasoline truck. There was an explosion and a fire."

"My God, Don't tell me anymore." "Hector is going to call you later." "I don't want to hear about it. I don't think I could take it." Jim was devastated. He couldn't speak. He just sat down and put his head his hands. Alex tried to comfort him, but it was no use. Finally, he got up and sped out of the parking lot. Alex ran after him calling "Jim, Jim." but he was out onto Route 110 in seconds. He drove straight to his house and laid down on the sofa and cried. He fell asleep. The phone rang several times but he refused to answer it. "Probably Alex." he thought. He didn't want to talk to anyone just then. Fate had dealt him another cruel blow.

The telephone rang and rang and rang. He refused to answer it. Then after several more rings, he picked up the phone only because it's incessant ringing was terribly annoying to him right now. "Hello." "Jim, this is the President of the United States." "Sir, I'm sorry, did you try calling before?" "We have been trying to get you for hours. I understand what is wrong. You have my sincere sympathy. I know the whole story about your friend Anne Fulton." "I wish there was something I could do to ease your grief." "Just your calling makes a tremendous difference. Sir""Jim, I know it's a bad time but we need you more than ever right now. The project is very serious and your friend Alex has informed us that the data is almost complete. Please return to the laboratory and help him." "This is a service to your country. We have to pay back that bastard for what he did at the World Trade Center." Jim straightened himself up and said "You're right Mr. President. This is bigger than any of our personal problems. I'm going back right now."

"Thank you, Jim and God Bless You. Ms. Fulton will be in my and my wife's prayers tonight."Jim made a call to Hector Thomson. Hector gave him the whole story of the accident. " There was an awful explosion and fire Jim." "We found her pocketbook about thirty yards away with her credit cards."

"Jim, she loved you and wanted to spend what little time she had with you, but it wasn't to be." "Does she have any family, I really didn't know much about her family. She told me she had a younger sister who was going to school in Edinburgh but that's all I knew." "She does have a sister who will be taking care of all the funeral arrangements." said Hector. "I won't even be able to make the funeral." said Jim.

"Wait. Maybe I can." Jim called the White House and spoke to Colin. "I need one day, to go to a funeral.""You've got it, Jim, one day won't kill us. As a matter of fact I'm way ahead of you. You can take the Concorde and be back the same day I'll make the arrangements."

Jim took the Concorde and attended the funeral for Anne. He met her sister, who looked a lot like a younger Ann. She was very kind to him. "Please call me Pam." she said after he addressed her as Ms .Fulton. They sat together at the church service. As he left she asked him if he would write to her and they could talk about Anne He said he would and got on the Concorde and was back at the laboratory the same day.

The information from "Investicom" was complete. It spewed out 330 pages. It indicated Longitudes and Latitudes of the frames on the tape, which also had images of Osama. A complete list was compiled and Jim called Washington. A Lear Jet was waiting for him at one of the private airports only a couple of miles from the lab. He got on board with his briefcase full of data for the Generals. The trip took only about thirty minutes and then he was taken by limousine to the White House. All in all the trip was just about an hour, door to door. The briefcase with the data was taken from him and dispatched by Marine courier to an unknown location in the Pentagon. Then they all waited as the information was analyzed.

They sat in a large conference room and the smoke from the cigarettes filled the air Coffee and cigarettes were the fair while they waited and waited. There was a large clock on the wall and Jim noted the time as he came in. They all sat in silence and occasionally Jim looked up at the clock. Then someone raised the volume on a TV set that hung from the wall. Bloomberg TV was giving the latest accounts on the Stock Market for the day. "Down again" said one of the Generals. There was a buzzer and it went off. The Admiral picked up an intercom and said "Yes, let him right in." In came a Marine Corps Sergeant with a briefcase. He saluted, made an about face and left the room, very militarily. The Admiral opened the briefcase and took out a leaf of papers. He went over them very slowly. When he was finished he looked up and said "Gentlemen, Mr. Feron's computer has given us over fifty locations in Afghanistan and Pakistan that Bin Laden was at when he taped these interviews. A good number of them we already knew about, but there are three new ones that could be of importance to our search. As a matter of fact one area could be just what we have been looking for. We are going to dispatch a team to that area to search. It happens to be one of the latest tapes that we came in possession of. Each of the Generals smiled and one went over and hugged Jim. He had tears in his eyes.

CHAPTER XVI

Jim would go to the area in Afghanistan, but first he had to undergo training with the USMC Force Recon. The USMC Recon's mission was to conduct pre- assault and distant post assault reconnaissance in support of a landing force, but most important was obtaining information on all routes, obstacles, terrain and enemy forces providing real time information through surveillance areas of interest and photographs and sketches to provide accurate visual aids describing areas and enemies. In addition, they possessed the capability to engage the enemy, implant sensors, capture prisoners and interrogate them. Jim spent a week in Quantico, Virginia with the USMC Recon units. They're a rugged lot and it took a lot for him to get through the training even though it was very short.

Once the training was over the team left for Egypt. It would be from there after a days rest that they would proceed to Afghanistan. The night they spent in Cairo was pleasant and they let it all hang out. They ate and drank and had fun for one night. The Marines were a rough lot and Jim got along very well with all of them, even though they were years younger than him.

The head of the team was a Major Bragg. He was about thirty two, six feet two inches tall and a trim one hundred and ninety pounds. He looked like he could fight a grizzly. He was very efficient and his men respected him. He gave the impression that he absolutely knew what he was doing.

The team was flown by transport to a staging area where tents had been set up. They would travel on foot about thirty miles to the area that they suspected where Osama had been at last.

The hike through the rugged terrain was no bargain, especially for Jim. However, Major Bragg gave sufficient break time through the hike. They took one break, where they all slept, but only for about four hours. They set up a perimeter guard and those picked to stand guard didn't get any sleep at all. They didn't seem to mind though. The hike was made mostly at night and without any machinery to make noise in case there were still members of Al- Qa'ida in the area. The Recon unit had a team of advanced scouts who hiked about five hundred yards ahead of the unit. They could see if there was any physical activity up ahead. They came to a hill and the scouts looked down into a valley, which had a barren flat area in front of a mountain range which they suspected had tunnels. The area matched the Longitude and Latitude analyzed from the tapes. They advised the team to stay back until they could determine if there were any inhabitants. It appeared that the area was abandoned but to make sure the waited until dark and then approached. They had night vision gear so they could see if there was any moving activity at all. There was none. They set up a camp and waited until daylight to explore fully. The men who had lost sleep due to sentry duty welcomed the chance to rest.

The next day, a search of the area began, but first proper shelters had to be erected. One tent for the men to sleep and another tent was erected as a sort of "office". Radio contact was made with the original staging area. The men had adequate supplies for food but more could be transported in by helicopter.

The search of the mountains was done with metal detectors and ultra violet sensors. On the second day a tunnel was discovered. It was well hidden. Before anyone entered the tunnel it was checked for booby traps and other devices that the Al- Qa'ida might have left. Satisfied that the area of the tunnel was secure, Major Bragg and Jim Feron entered the tunnel. One advantage that they had by adding Jim Feron to the team was his expertise in "traps" and hidden rooms or passages. He had worked with a Detective in the District Attorney's Office who besides being a lock picker and a wiretap installation expert was also adept at finding hiding places that the mob used in their cars, homes and offices for guns, money and drugs. He had passed along his expertise to Jim. Jim went along the walls of the cave searching for some little device that might trigger a mechanism opening up a new passageway. Outside, a team of men were going over the grounds searching with other metal detectors and some new electronic devices that were Top Secret, which could disclose footprints or tire marks some ten feet below the ground. Jim felt along the walls with his hands and suddenly looked up and saw a suspicious group of stones sitting on a groove in the wall that looked like a shelf. He removed the stones and there was an electronic switch. He called Major Bragg over to look. They both decided that everyone would leave the tunnel except for Jim and the Major, just in case it was a booby trap. After all of the team had left the tunnel and were safely away from it's entrance, they stood with their back firmly placed against the walls of the tunnel. They remained in radio contact with the team outside. The Major gave the word "Go ahead Jim, Hit the switch." Jim hit the switch and held his breath. Nothing happened. He hit it again and they both heard a sound like gears and wheels turning. The wall opened up. It was a very cleverly hid entrance. The cracks in the entrance having been filled with clay and dirt so as not to reveal the door. The door was operated by a battery which fortunately still had some life in it. Behind the door was a passageway which led to a room. The room was about 16 feet by 20 feet. The room had a computer, a desk and some file cabinets. The file cabinets had been emptied as it seemed very hurriedly. There was a shredding machine with some residue of shredded paper still in it. The computer had been disabled. There was a locker and inside the locker were a pair of shoes. They were "Beal Brothers". They had struck treasure.

The shredded papers were removed and a helicopter was dispatched to take them to the staging area. In hours they would be in Washington with FBI technicians going over them to piece the shredded documents back together so that they could be interpreted.

Fortunately the shredder was not one of those that shredded into confetti type residue, but an older type that shredded into strips. The computer and the"boots" were also sent to the FBI laboratory for analysis. Everything that was sent to Washington was replaced with duplicates. Duplicate computers, shredding machines, the locker and even another set of "Beal Brothers" boots. All of these items were returned to Bragg's team so that if the Taliban returned, they would not know that their camp had been uncovered.

Meanwhile Jim, Major Bragg and the team continued their work in the area. The sensors had detected some tire prints in one flat clean area. A whole range of photographs were made of the tire marks. The tire mark photos were scanned into Major Bragg's lap top and sent by E-mail through a secure site to the lab also. They all had been working for almost twenty hours and were pretty tired. The team needed some rest and recreation. Major Bragg gave the word for the men to set up some barbecue stoves and then they would have a steak fry. The steaks were brought by helicopter accompanied by beer. Each man was allowed three cans of beer and a huge steak. To go with the steak, they also had frozen packages of french fried potatoes and onion rings. The men all enjoyed their feast and then "hit the sack" except of course for the sentries. The sentry duty was broken up into two hour tours which gave everyone a better rest.

They all awoke with the sunrise and Major Bragg summoned Jim and his officers and non-commissioned officers for a meeting in the office tent. The information being analyzed would take about two days. In the mean time they would maintain the camp. There would be exercise drills in the morning and after sun down. The men would take turns running the mess and the guard duty. At night, there would be a movie played on a 72 inch television set with a VCR for anyone who wanted to attend. Otherwise there were card tables and the rest of the men could play cards or checkers or chess. There would be no gambling. This would help to pass the time until the information came in from Washington.

The men were in the middle of their early morning workout, when they heard the whirring noise of a helicopter overhead. It set down and a Marine Sergeant got out with a briefcase which he took directly to Major Bragg's tent. He was seen saluting, doing an about face and double timing back to the helicopter which took right off.

The men all waited nervously until Bragg announced over a bull horn that there would be a meeting in his tent in one hour. They were all seated around an oval table with Bragg at the head of the table. He had a sheaf of papers in front of him. "Gentlemen , we have news. We have found a camp that undoubtedly was used by Bin Laden. The Beal Boots appeared to have been his. The analysis of the ground show tire tracks used by a Lear Jet. The shredded material has been analyzed and marked "Top Secret". "At this time I am the only one allowed to know the contents." His face took on a very stern, serious look when he spoke of the shredded papers. One officer stood up ."Sir, I don't mean to question, but are the papers material to our finding Bin Laden and why......"

The Major cut him off "Let's just say that they do not help find him and they are meant for only a few eyes at this time."There are indications that the Lear Jet took Bin Laden from here and landed in Saudi Arabia. Intelligence tells us that he possibly was taken to a hospital for kidney dialysis and also a broken arm. Information has leaked out of Arabia that a bearded man was brought into a hospital in the southern part of Arabia and treated. He was well guarded and the hospital staff was kept away from him. A separate staff came into the hospital to treat this man. It is believed that one of Bin Laden's Saudi Prince friends made all the arrangements including the transportation by Jet. One of our aircraft carriers is sitting in the Persian Gulf flying AWACS around the clock hoping to find a Lear flying out of southern Saudi Arabia, should he attempt to come back to Afghanistan."

"What are we going to do now?" said one of the men." We are going to stand down until we receive further orders from Washington." "We are scheduled to stay here for at least two weeks." "One thing, though, we are going to need to move our equipment into one of the tunnels so that we cannot be detected from the air or any ground forces." "We will do this immediately." The team started dismantling the tents and all of the electronic equipment and moving it into a tunnel that was alongside the one that apparently was used by Bin Laden. The whole move took twenty four hours and when it was done, all traces of the former camp were systematically erased. It was done so efficiently that no one would have ever known that there was a camp there before.

Bragg inspected the area and he was well pleased with the results of the "erasure".Now all they could do was to wait for two weeks.

During the two weeks, Jim spent his evenings in pleasant conversation with Major Bragg. They got to be very close. Bragg and Jim exchanged "war stories". Bragg about his experiences during Desert Storm and Jim about his many cases that he worked in he Police Department. Bragg was a very humble individual and although he had been involved in some serious operations during Desert Storm, he was very interested in the operations of the Detective Division of the New York City Police Department. He would ask so many questions. It was clear that he was a "buff". "The only contact I ever had with the Police operations was through television." "The way you describe it is so different." Jim relished telling him some of the more intricate investigations he worked on. He thought to himself "I would have loved to have this guy as a partner on the job."

Jim told him the sad story of his wife and children's kidnapping. Bragg said "And you've never found out what happened to them?" "No." I had one chance to capture the man who I believe was responsible and I muffed it." Bragg had a tragic story to tell. He told of how his wife was a Navy nurse and contracted AIDS treating a drug addict. " She stuck her hand in his trousers to empty his belongings and got stuck with a needle. " She lived for a year and then succumbed to the disease." " She was only twenty-eight years old." "Any children?" said Jim. "No we wanted to have some but we waited too long." "I am going out with a gal right now, who is also a Navy nurse and we plan to get married next year." "I hope you'll invite me." "You will be right up there on the invitation list." "We plan to marry in her home town in Pennsylvania." "I'm looking forward to it." said Jim.

The two weeks went by very slowly for the team. They were all ready for some action and there was none , at least for now. They were at "chow" when they got the alert. A unit, suspected of being Al Qa'ida was proceeding toward their area. The tunnel was closed up the way it had been originally and the team disbursed to locations where they could observe entrance of any force to the area. They were pretty well camouflaged and ready. The force came in with three truckloads of men. They were well armed. The soldiers had 7.62 mm Machine Guns and some of the leaders carried 7.62 Tokarev Pistols. They also had some Sa-7 Grail, man portable SAMs (Surface to Air Missiles).

The word was passed along that no attack was to be started. They just sat and watched. They watched into the night and then they watched through "night vision" binoculars. The Taliban force reestablished themselves inside the tunnels. The tunnels had been neatly restored to their former state. Inside the disabled computers and the shredding machine were just the way they had been left They even had the locker put back with the boots inside.

The Taliban force apparently bought the deception, because they moved into the tunnel without any apparent suspicions.

The next morning after sunrise, Major Bragg was notified by radio. A Lear Jet was heading toward the area. He passed the word along to his men. Jim and Major Bragg looked at each other, each one thinking the same thing " Could he be on that plane?" Then they saw the Jet. It circled and came in down wind. There was a perfectly flat piece of ground for it to land. This was exactly where the Marines had located the tire marks using their Top Secret equipment.

The Lear Jet taxied to a stop surrounded by machine gun toting soldiers, who formed s semi circle around the passenger door. The door opened and a bearded man stepped out. He was paid homage by the group. They bowed. They blessed themselves in the traditional Islamic fashion. He returned the blessing. There was no mistaking. It was Bin Laden. He looked pale and had a cane. His one arm was in a sling. He did have a pistol belt around his waist. He was led from the plane to the tunnel. Major Bragg kept watch while everyone waited for his instructions.

Major Bragg assembled his officers behind the hill that they were using to observe the Taliban's operations. "We want to capture him alive, at all costs."

CHAPTER XVII

Alex lit a cigar and sat down with a glass of Courvoisier Brandy. He was tired. He hadn't heard anything from Jim in almost three weeks. "I wonder how he is?" He was worried. He didn't want to lose his partner. He doubted if he could ever get someone as dedicated as Jim was. He heard the sound of a helicopter outside the laboratory. It was a courier with a message for him. The Marine Sergeant dressed in fatigues gave him a smart salute and presented him with a folder. "I need you to sign for this, sir, Mr Lermindov." "How do you know my name, Soldier?" "I was shown your photograph, sir." Alex thanked the Sergeant as he signed for the package. "Safe trip back, Soldier." "The name is Sergeant Tyme, sir and I'm a United States Marine." "I beg your pardon, I know how proud you people are of your service." The folder contained a message from William Colin. It about Jim Feron. He was alright and engaged in a serious operation which was Top Secret. That's all it said. "They sent a helicopter all the way just to tell me this bullshit." said Lermindov to himself. Still, he was happy to know that as of yesterday Jim was still safe.

Alex Lermindov was busy researching a new investigative tool that he felt would be invaluable if used by "Investicom" The program was called Facial Recognition. It was already being implemented in the casinos in Las Vegas. They were able to identify known cheats even though they had disguised themselves. The system mapped the face , plotting the angles and plateaus of the face just as orbiting satellites did to map the earth. It concentrated on the shape of the face, avoiding hair color and length. In addition, weight gain or loss had no effect on the identification. The mathematical measurements of the face are tied to the individuals photo or from a video image. This information is put into a database and can be compared to other photos or videos. "God, this is like the Bertillon system only so much better." In the days before fingerprints , a system known as the Bertillon system was used by law enforcement. Bertillon, who was a bureaucrat and the son and brother of physicians who had strong interests in the collection and interpretation of medical statistics developed and implemented his system while he was the Chief of Identification of the Paris Police. After years of experimentation, Bertillon utilized his system of Criminal Identification in 1882 . He used it on Criminal Offenders that were detained at the Paris Palace of Justice. Bertillon's method was to photograph the subject having him look directly into the camera and then take another photo of the subject's profile with the camera centered upon the subject's right ear. He would measure the subject's height, along with the length of one foot, an arm and an index finger.

Bertillon's techniques proved to be so useful that elements of his system are still being used by Police Departments and other authorities throughout the world. "Someone has utilized the theory and gone much further." thought Lermindov. Alex put through a telephone call to one of the casinos in Las Vegas that was currently using "Facial Recognition. An article in the Las Vegas newspaper described how they had identified a notorious card cheat and had him expelled from their casino. Alex spoke with the Security Chief of Aladdin's Magic Carpet, one of the largest casinos in Vegas. The Security Chief happened to be a former Los Angeles Department Police Captain. His name was James Lane. He was very cordial to Alex. "I know your partner, Jim Feron." " I met him when I was in the Department." "I had to go to New York , We held a group seminar on Intelligence. We bent a few elbows together." " Where is he now?" "I can't say, he is doing some work for the government and they won't even tell me where he is."

"If there is anything I can help you with please feel free." said Lane. "The only thing is that there are several companies that have the patent on this system and you would have to get their permission to use it." "Naturally they will want to be paid for their system. I don' t even know if they would allow you to incorporate their system into your computer." Alex said "I know, this could be a problem, however , I have a lot of weight behind me and we might be able to swing a Government contract for them." Lane gave Alex the names of the companies in Minnesota, Wisconsin and Massachusetts that he could contact. "Thank you my friend, I will tell Jim to give you a call when he comes back." "Please do that." said Lane.

The Government contract for the Facial Recognition program was quickly approved and Alex worked on downloading it into "Investicom"

Alex got a call from Jimmy Lane right after they got the contract. Lane told him about a "cheat" that they had spotted, who was identified by the Facial Recognition program. He was in the middle of a poker game and had won several thousand dollars. They had no trouble grabbing a identifying him, but he had an accomplice, who they had never seen before and he managed to slip out of the casino before they could grab him. "We got a full face photo of him and some video so if he ever comes in again, we'll get him." Alex told

Lane to send him the photos and video of the accomplice and he would run them through "Investicom". "Thanks, Alex, may I call you Alex or should I call you Professor."

"Call me Alex." "I'll get those photos right out to you."Alex received the photos and the video the next day by Fed Ex. Alex ran the photos and the video through the computer and waited for the results. The computer would search all the photo files that it had. The most important of which were Police Department photos from throughout the United States. The search would take a few hours and in the meantime, Alex put in a movie in his VCR. He had a favorite. It was Dr. Zhivago. The movie was quite long and he had come to the scene in the movie where Zhivago sees Lara from the window of a trolley and attempts to catch up to her, but he suffers a heart attack in the process of the chase. "How sad." said Alex even though he had seen the movie four or five times before. He had always hoped that Zhivago would catch up with Lara, but it never happens. The search was completed and "Investicom" had come up with a match. Alex's eyes lit up as he read the data with the two photos. One from Lane and the matching one from "Investicom" He had a brandy in his hand and was sipping it while he looked over the data. He nearly choked. He spit up the brandy and he dropped the "snifter". His hands were shaking. The match was Brian Ferguson.

So Brian Ferguson was in Las Vegas. He called Jim Lane and told him about the match."It figures, because the other guy is Irish and has been linked to some IRA terrorists." "You guys have got to find him." said Alex. He kidnaped Jim Feron's wife years ago and he is the only link we have to finding out what happened to Jim's wife and kids." "I know all about that story." "I'll get the best guys out here working on it." "I'll get back soon."

Two days later, Brian Ferguson walked into one of the other casinos and was identified by the Facial Recognition program. The Security Director called Lane who was only two blocks away in "Aladdin's Magic Carpet." He in turn called the Las Vegas Police and they blocked off the entrance to the casino. Ferguson was being surveilled from a private room used by the Security Personnel. Two plainclothes officers walked slowly toward were Ferguson was seated playing a slot machine. They pinned him to the machine and attempted to handcuff him. He was very strong and he broke free and started to run down the aisles of the slots. He knocked over an old lady who had a bucket filled with quarters. They went flying. When he reached the door, he realized that he was trapped so he stopped and turned and drew out an automatic. The officers were afraid to shoot because there were so many people in the casino so they just pointed their weapons at him. He fired at one officer and brought him down. An officer behind him decided that he had a clear shot and he fired hitting Ferguson squarely between the shoulder blades. He went down squirting blood. They took no chances and disarmed him and cuffed him on the floor. An ambulance was summoned and a trail of police cars and the ambulance sped to the local hospital. The officer who was shot was driven in a second ambulance. They all arrived at the Emergency Entrance at the same time and Ferguson was taken into Surgery One and the Vegas Policemen went into Surgery Two. Alex was notified of the capture and told that Ferguson was in Intensive Care and they didn't think he was going to make it. "How long do you think he has?" "I don't know" said Lane. "Maybe a day, maybe only hours." Alex wanted very much to have a chance to interrogate Ferguson but he couldn't leave the laboratory without getting permission. He called Colin and explained it to him. Colin dispatched a Jet to the lab and then Lermindov was flown to Las

Vegas Airport. He got to the hospital where he was met by Jim Lane. " I don't know how much longer, he'll be around." said Jim. "The doctor is in with him right now."

"We'll know as soon as he comes out." The doctor came out and spoke with Lane and Alex. "He has maybe a half hour at best." "He wants a priest." Alex looked at the doctor in dismay. "That son of a bitch wants a priest?" "It has something to do with a promise to his mother. He told her that if he ever was dying he would confess to a priest before he went."

"We've sent for one from St. Michael's Church. If you want to talk to him, do it now. Once the priest gets here I have to let him in," Alex asked to go in alone and Jim agreed. He sat down next to Ferguson, who had his eyes closed. "Ferguson, open your eyes, it's an old friend." Ferguson opened his eyes and with a smirk said "Fuck you Russian"

"Talk to me Ferguson, you are going to die anyway. Tell me about Feron's wife and kids."

"Where's the priest, they promised me a priest. Me old mother, I promised her I wouldn't die without the sacraments." There was a knock on the door. Alex went to the door. It was Father O'Brien from St. Michaels. Alex told him to wait. "Listen Father I need a couple of more minutes." He went back to the bed and tried with Ferguson again. "Where's the priest. Was that him?" "I sent him away." "I won't let him give you the sacraments unless you talk to me." Ferguson now had a look of panic on his face. "You can't do that, I'm entitled to be seen by a priest." "What do I care what you're entitled to." "Sue me, put me in jail, write a letter to your congressman." "You talk to me or you'll die and go straight to hell, where you belong."

"Okay, okay," said Ferguson in a dry raspy voice. "I'll tell you. After we took the wife and kids .,,,," and he started to cough. "We took them to a safe house." "The woman was afraid that we would rape her so somehow she took some pills, sleeping pills, a whole lot of them. She had them in her bag. Stupid bastards, we didn't search her." "She went into convulsions and died on us." "What about the children?" Alex was getting impatient. "The kids, ..." he coughed again. "The kids were taken to Canada" "We sold them to a family, who had none." "What was the name of the family in Canada?" said Alex. Now he was coughing uncontrollably and spitting up. "What was the name of the family?" Alex asked again. "Mc ....something." "McPherson" "It was Angus and Josie McPherson" ."They lived in Ontario." He started to cough again and Alex realizing that this was all he was going to get out of him, went outside and summoned the priest Ferguson's mother got her wish and he died. Alex wondered to himself "I wonder if he has saved his soul after all the evil that he did?" Alex went out and told Lane what happened. Alex had to go back as soon as possible.

The Jet was waiting for him courtesy of William Colin. He bid Lane Goodbye and flew back. Alex could not wait to put the McPherson into the computer. He tried every available program that they had for finding families. The computer could check a family history like no other. He got a lot of information relative McPherson. Which one was the one with Jim's children and where were they now.

Angus and Josie McPherson initially lived in a suburb of the eastern end of Ontario and then moved to Windsor, Ontario. From their credit reports, they seemed to be in a lot of financial difficulties. The father worked as a miner and the mother was a teacher. They were in Windsor for about ten years and then it appears that the old man died leaving the mother and the two children. But it didn't mention the kids. The mother retired from teaching and the last documentation showed them living in Windsor on Lake Drive. Alex made a call to the Windsor, Ontario Police Department. He got a name from Jim's old American Society for Industrial Security Directory Book. He called the contact. It was a Detective in the Windsor Police Department. A Detective Kitchener . Alex explained the whole story to him and the Detective listened very intently. He was no slouch. He told Alex he would contact the Windsor Educational Department and find out if Mrs. McPherson was collecting pension checks and where were they being sent. He would call him back when he had some news. Kitchener called back with some news. Mrs. McPherson was collecting checks or rather the checks were being sent to a Nursing Home outside of Windsor. Kitchener was on his way there to interview Mrs. McPherson. Alex was excited. He waited in laboratory for a call back Alex fell asleep on a couch in the lab. He couldn't stay awake. It was close to 1:00 A.M. when he finally dozed off. The phone rang at 8:00 AM and Alex stirred from his deep sleep. It was Kitchener and he had good news. Mrs. McPherson was in the Nursing Home and he spoke with her. She confirmed that she and her husband had bought two children from some "not so nice" Irishmen, as she called them. But she and her husband wanted children desperately and they gave all of their savings to these men. "Five Thousand dollars" she said "Every cent we had." "They told me if I made any inquiries as to the identity of the children, that I would lose them." "We kept our mouths shut and raised two beautiful kids." Kitchener went on "You won't believe this but while I was there the boy, I mean man came in to visit his mom." Alex said "You mean you saw Jim's son?" "And not only that the daughter was coming tomorrow, I mean today. And I will see her also.""They know that they were adopted and when I spoke to the son, he was very excited about finding out about his biological father." Alex started to cry. "Wait until I tell Jim, I can't wait."

"Where the hell is that son of a bitch?" The next day Alex received a phone call from both of them. They asked a hundred questions. All he could tell them was that their father was working for the Government and would return very soon. He would have him call them as soon as he returned. They were very impatient. They wanted to fly to New York, but Alex told them to wait because their father's itinerary was "kind of secret" and he really didn't know when he would be back. They agreed to wait, but only after he promised to call them as soon as Jim came back. This was the good news, but the bad news was their old nemesis Congresswoman Hilton had learned that "Investicom" had been used by Alex for personal reasons and in addition, the President's advisor had authorized the use of a Government plane for personal reasons also. William Colin had to explain why this was done. He appeared before a Congressional Committee and he spoke. He was allowed to speak uninterruptedly for thirty minutes.

"Congressmen and Congresswomen, I come to this committee today to tell you that I have used a Government plane for a civilian's use. I would like to tell you a story. This is a story of dedication and grief. It is the story of a breakthrough in law enforcement, the likes of which no one will ever see again." He went on to tell of Jim Feron"s family and how they were kidnapped. He related how he (Feron) had since dedicated himself with his colleague, Alex Lermindov to build the world's greatest computer for locating people. He told them of the cases of Mary Grey. Then he told them how the United States had helped one it's Allies locate a Member of their Parliament who had been missing. A very important MP with access to super secret information. Then after documenting the cases that "Investicom" had solved, he told how Alex Lermindov had decided on his own to use the computer to solve a seventeen year old mystery. That of the disappearance of Jim Feron's wife and children. "This man works for us. Could we deny him the chance to help his friend an colleague.""Okay, he didn't get permission, but he felt that he couldn't wait." " His only sin in this matter was his impatience." "If he is guilty, then so am I, for letting him use the Jet."

After Colin's testimony, the Chairman of the Committee thanked him and told him that they would meet in camera and let him know their finding of the charges of misuse of Government equipment.

The Committee met after lunch and it didn't take them long to decide to drop the matter. It was a heated session, with one of the Congressmen standing up and shaking his fist in the air. "We cannot punish men like this. They are the most patriotic of patriotic people in this country and their work is paramount to our Criminal Justice system." Some of the members of the Committee applauded while the Chairman called for order. After that there was no question that there would be no findings of misconduct.

Alex was notified by Colin that there would be no charges of misconduct against either of them. He thanked Colin and said "They don't know what a good man they have in office helping the President." "Can't we get in touch with Jim and let him know that we've found his children?" Colin replied "I'd like nothing better but let me tell you Alex, he is at such a critical stage in the mission that to tell him might distract him from what he is doing and jeopardize the mission and also jeopardize his safety so please trust me when I say I cannot tell him anything right now." "I trust you implicitly, sir." said Alex.

CHAPTER XVIII

Major Bragg had formulated the plan to attack the tunnel. It would be a night time operation. The outside of the tunnel was guarded by four Taliban soldiers. There was a small fire burning in front of the tunnel entrance. The tunnel entrance now visible, had a steel door. The guards were observed from the top of a hill by night vision binoculars. The plan was simply this. The guards would be taken out by dart guns loaded with a strong anesthesia. They would be taken down simultaneously. Once this was done two squads would drill a hole in the tunnel and pump in CS gas. CS stood for Chlorobenzalmalononitrile, which was a white powder and when mixed with a dispersal agent like methylene chloride, enabled it to be carried through the air. Physical aspects of this tear gas were burning of the eyes, an involuntary closing of the eyes, burning of the nose, coughing, nausea . Recovery is effected by exposure to fresh air. Then they would blow open the door with explosive charges and charge inside. Whatever Taliban forces were inside would be ushered out to be taken prisoner by another squad outside. The other squads would search inside for Bin Laden.

The operation got under way. Bragg gave the word to disable the guards. Marine Snipers with dart guns fired and successfully took down the guards. The other squads drilled a hole into the tunnel and the CS was then pumped into the tunnel through spray nozzles which were pumped by CEV's (Combat Engineering Vehicles). This was similar to the operation that the FBI employed at Waco, during the Branch Davidian siege.

The two squads entering the tunnel donned their gas masks as the door was blown away. The steel door flew from it's position in front of the tunnel. The men stood far enough back so as not to be injured by the explosion and the flying steel door. Bragg was one of the first inside the tunnel. Jim was right along side of him. Two large headlights were put into operation, illuminating the inside. Jim and Bragg went directly to the secret room, the one that Jim had found with the hidden trigger mechanism. Marines were pushing disoriented Taliban outside of the tunnel. They entered the "office" room and there were some Taliban staggering around in there. They were quickly taken prisoner. Bragg and Jim looked in every corner of the room. "Look here said Bragg." He pointed to a door which apparently led to the outside. "He's escaped." he said. They ran out the door and to the outside of the cave in time to see two men mounting horses. One turned and fired at them.

Bragg took him down with one shot from his AK47. He refrained from shooting at the other man for obvious reasons.

"It's him, he's getting away." There were two horses outside. The man that Bragg shot fell off one horse and there was a second one tied up to a pole, which was probably for a second body guard of Bin Laden who never made it out of the tunnel. Bragg mounted one horse and Jim the other and took off after Bin Laden.

It was like a scene out of an old western movie. Bin Laden galloping across the desert with Bragg and Jim behind him. Just like an old Hopalong Cassidy flick thought Jim as they pursued their "bad guy". Bragg was an accomplished horseman and he began to close the distance between him and Bin Laden. Jim, unfortunately was not and he lagged behind.

Bragg came alongside of Bin Laden and pulled him down as they both came off of their mounts and hit the ground very hard. Bin Laden rolled and then was up in an instant facing Bragg with a pistol. Bragg very quickly sprang to his feet and he too drew a pistol. They faced each other for what seemed forever, before Bin Laden fired first. Striking Bragg in the hip. It was not enough though to prevent Bragg from firing also. Only he fired a volley all from a crouched position similar to ones used by law enforcement officers at their firing ranges. He hit Bin Laden six times. He didn't miss a shot. Bin Laden's chest exploded with the hits. He hit the ground and was dead instantly. Jim pulled up just as the shooting ended.

"I wanted him alive. The son of a bitch cheated us." "You're bleeding" and Jim pulled out a compress from a small kit on his belt. "I'm alright, Jim, but I've screwed up the whole deal by killing him." "You had no choice, It was him or you." Jim said as he applied the compress.

The body of Bin Laden was brought back to the area and then transported back to the staging area to be taken from there to the United States, where a complete verification of his identity was to be made. The Marines had rounded up all of the Taliban, who were now starting to recover from the CS attack. They were herded into tents and searched and had all of their clothing removed and then they were given orange jump suits to put on. All of their clothing and belongings would be thoroughly gone over for any hidden weapons or any papers useful to Intelligence.

Operation Bin Laden was over.

CHAPTER XIX

When Tom Bragg and Jim Feron arrived in Washington, they were taken to the same conference room where it had all started with the Generals and the Admiral. Bill Colin chaired the meeting. First Major Bragg gave his account of the mission and when he was finished he apologized to the military for his failure to apprehend Bin Laden alive. Jim then told his side of the story and he was full of praise and admiration for the way in which Bragg handled it. He said ""I am proud to have been a part of this operation and this man did everything in his power to capture Bin Laden alive almost at the cost of his own life." "He allowed Bin Laden to fire first, which fortunately only wounded him." "He even hesitated after that before firing." The Generals listened and then one of them, the Marine Corps General spoke. "Mr. Colin, may I read the forensic report on the deceased "Bin Laden" to our two gentlemen?" "Be my guest, General."

General Stock opened a folder marked "Top Secret" and started to read the Autopsy Report on the deceased man that Bragg had killed. "The man was about 45 years of age, 6'4" tall, and weighed 163 pounds. He had brown hair, brown eyes and an olive complexion. He appeared to be left handed, however forensic tests of his teeth comparing them to records obtained from Saudi Arabia indicate that the teeth were not that of Bin Laden. Another inconsistency was that the blood type was different from Bin Laden's. The report goes on about scars and moles on the body which do not match those known on Bin Laden. "Gentlemen, we did not kill Osama Bin Laden. We have apparently killed a double." " Osama Bin Laden is still alive as far as we know."

"On behalf of this committee, I want to commend Major Bragg and of course former New York City Police Detective James Feron for his part in the operation." "I have recommended that Major Bragg be awarded the "Bronze Star" and all though Mr. Feron is a civilian we have cleared with the Congress for him to receive this decoration also." "These awards and the entire operation is considered Top Secret and no part of the operation will be leaked out to the press. As far as we are concerned it never happened." "I believe we are all in agreement that if any of the operation were leaked to the press it could compromise "Investicom" and it would be fodder for making us look foolish, although no one could have known that Mr. Bin Laden had a "double". Admiral Pine spoke "He doesn't have a double any more." This brought a chuckle to the table. Colin now got up and said "Gentlemen this meeting is adjourned and the President will be personally advised by me of the proceedings., If there is any reason to reconvene , you will all be notified." "I understand that Congratulations are in order for Major Bragg who is getting married next week or have you changed the date again, Tom?" " No sir, it's set for next week and you are all invited, although I realize that you probably won't be able to attend but thank you anyway." "But you are coming aren't you." he said directly to Jim." "I wouldn't miss it for the world." The meeting broke up and Bragg and Jim split up. Bragg goingto the BOQ quarters in Quantico and Jim to a hotel in

D.C. They would meet for a drink later on. Jim was anxious to talk to Alex and as soon as he got settled in at the hotel he placed a call to the laboratory.

Alex was not at the lab, and he was not home either. Jim left messages on both of his voice mails and then took a shower and left to have his drink with Tom Bragg. He was really looking forward to having a few with Tom. They had been through a lot and he really liked the guy. He figured that Alex was probably relaxing and anyway he didn't know that what Alex had to tell him would knock his socks off.

Tom and Jim relaxed with a few drinks at a piano bar in the hotel. They sang along with the music. "Their breaking up that old gang of mine." they sang and then "Can't take my eyes offa you." just like from "Deer Hunter" " Did you see that picture, Tom?" "Yeah, I did, and I was in Vietnam. What bullshit."

" When they captured a prisoner, they just killed them, none of that Russian Roulette crap." They passed war stories back and forth and laughed and drank and finally decided that it was time to go to bed. Tom was going back to the BOQ and then would meet his prospective bride tomorrow and the wedding would take place in a couple of days. Jim said he would stay on til the wedding. They hugged and both staggered away to their respective locations.

Jim was awakened the next day by the phone. He had a headache and his stomach felt a little queasy. It was Alex. "Alex, I'm so glad to hear your voice." "What's new?"Jim had no way of knowing that what was new would knock him on his back. "Jim." "Are you sitting down?" "Yeah, don't play games with me I've got a terrible hangover, Been celebrating.""Jim, I really don't know how to start, but I've found your children." There was a long pause of silence. "What are you saying Alex?" "I've found your children, While you were gone we got lucky and I'm kind of mixed up. I don't know how to start." "Start" said Jim. Alex related story of how they had found Brian Ferguson and the chase and capture and the subsequent interrogation in the hospital. Jim listened intently without saying a word.

Alex told him that the kids wanted to speak to their father and he had to tell them to wait until Jim returned. Jim then wanted to know when he could talk to them.

"Today." said Alex. He would call them and have them call Jim at the hotel. He told Alex that he would not move from the spot until they called.

He had his breakfast sent to the room and he just sat and thought about his wife and that terrible day when he lost all of them. He said a silent prayer to St. Anthony. "I know you had something to do with finding them." he said to himself. Again he sat alone waiting for one of the most important calls of his life. He was on his second cup of coffee when they called. First he spoke to his daughter, Ann. "Daddy, it's been so long and I have so much to tell you." "First, how are you?" he said."When can we see each other?" "We'll spend time and you can tell me all the things you are doing and did in the past seventeen years." "Let's see, you must be about twenty, twenty-one, right?""I am twenty-one this past week."

"Oh when I see you we'll celebrate your birthday." "Did you keep your name Ann or did you get a new one?" "My name is Elizabeth and I understand that's my real mom's name." "Dad, I can't really remember how we parted, It's all very vague to me. John, I mean Jim, my brother he remembers it better." "John, did he take the name John?" "Yes. They named him John."Elizabeth and Jim spoke for a half hour and her brother John waited patiently for his turn. "What are you doing right now, I mean do you work or go to school?" asked Feron. "I work. I work doing Computer

Programming." "Oh wow have I got a lot to talk to you about." he said. "Dad, John is tugging at me now, he wants so badly to talk to you. So I'll put him on." "But first I want to let you know we are coming to Long Island next week to see you. " " That's wonderful." said Jim

"I'm going to a wedding here and I'll be back in Long Island on Tuesday." "We'll be there on Thursday, ... Dad." "Dad, I love you." "Love you too darling." and he wiped a tear away. John got on the phone with his father and he was so emotional that at first he could not speak just stutter and cry. "It's okay son, just take it easy and talk to me." John spoke very slowly about the kidnapping. He remembered it. " After they kidnapped us, they drove for hours. It seemed like about a whole day." "They took us to a house in the woods and put us in separate rooms. I heard Mom getting sick and a lot of noise and then they carried her out. She was dead. They buried her behind the house." "One of the men complained about what to do with us. I think he wanted to kill us, but the other said he had an idea of how to make some bucks."

"Then we were taken to this farm and that's when they sold us to the McPherson family." "At first I cried and tried to escape, but each time they brought me back and finally after a while, I, we didn't mind it there. They were very nice to us and somehow we went to school. The first day at school I tried to tell the teacher that I was kidnapped but she didn't believe me." "Thought I had a great imagination." she said. I am studying Forensic Pathology and I even got to intern in Long Island, when Flight 800 went down." Jim couldn't believe his ears. His son had been on Long Island, no further than a few miles from the lab. After talking for over an hour, they decided to wait until they could see each other face to face and spend some time together. John said "Dad, I love you, Let's not have anything separate us again." "I can't wait until next week." "Neither can I." said Jim. Jim hung up the phone and then kind of collapsed on the bed. He was physically and mentally drained. But a smile crossed his face as he went into a deep sleep. He was dreaming again about Elizabeth and the kids. Then in his dream Anne appeared and he introduced her to Elizabeth. "Elizabeth, this is Anne Fulton, I met her in Scotland." "I know." said Elizabeth. "It's alright Jim, I understand."

Then he just slept and slept. When he woke up it was about four in the afternoon.He wa s hungry again so he went down to the restaurant and had an early supper. But first he had a couple of drinks at the bar. Tom Bragg called him after his supper. He was in the middle of watching a Turner Classic Movie. Dr. Zhivago was on. He watched some of it and thought of Alex. He figured on going to bed early but when Tom called he became wide awake. Tom told him that the arrangements for the wedding were all done. The wedding would be performed in the Chapel in Quantico and then the reception was to be held at the Officers Club. "Jim, my brother was supposed to be my Best Man when we originally planned this but he works for the Agency and is on some kind of job and can't get back in time, so I want you to kind of be his proxy." "Would you do that for me?" "I, I don't know what to say." "This is such an honor." "Of course I'll stand in for your brother." Tom Bragg could tell from Jim's voice that he was getting emotional."Hey, you're not going to cry on me now are you?" Jim didn't answer. Then he asked if he should get a tuxedo. "It's all taken care of, you go to the Post Exchange on the base and they will fit you for a rental tux." "Boy, you were pretty sure I'd say yes, weren't you?" "I was not about to take no for an answer, Mr. Feron " Jim stood up at the altar alongside of Tom Bragg, when the bride walked up the aisle towards them escorted by her father, who was a Navy Captain.

"Gosh, isn't she beautiful, Jim." whispered Tom to Jim. "Shhhh" said Jim and gave him a nudge with his elbow. The Navy Chaplain, Father Riley performed the ceremony. They exchanged their rings and he pronounced them Man and Wife. Tom gave Monica, his bride a soft kiss and then they smiled at each other and walked down the aisle and then under an overhead of Officers' sabers.

The reception was a blast. Tom and Monica sat under a canopy of flowers and drank champagne. They danced and danced. Jim got up and made the toast. " He picked up a bottle of champagne and as he toasted he pointed the bottle first at Monica, then at Tom and lastly at himself. "Here's to a sweetheart a bottle and a friend" "The first beautiful, the second full and the last ever faithful."

"May you have warm words on a cool evening, a full moon on a dark night and may the road be downhill all the way to your door." Then he addressed the guests.

"Here's health to all those we love, here's health to all those that love us. Here's health to all those that love them, that love those, that love them, that love us." and everyone cheered. Tom introduced Jim to Monica's sister, Linda, who was the Maid of Honor. She was a Navy nurse like her sister. She was in her late thirties and a clearly attractive woman. Jim danced with her when the wedding party was introduced and when they all retreated to their tables, he whispered to her. "You're a wonderful dancer, I hope you'll honor me with another." "You bet." she said ""I might not dance with anyone else." It turned out that they were seated next to each other at a table just to the right of the bride and groom. They danced and they talked and found that they liked the same things. Linda had been married and divorced. Jim wondered how anyone could break up with such a pleasant woman. Linda told him that her husband was in the military and they were separated too many times and when he was away he apparently got lonely and took up with other women. She could not take his infidelity, so they divorced. Jim was reluctant to tell her about his misfortune with his wife and children. He merely told her that his wife was dead. He never mentioned the children. As he spoke with her, his thoughts drifted to his children and how he longed to see them again. "Penny for your thoughts." she said.

"Oh, they're worth so much more than that." "Sometime when we know each other better, I'll sell them to you for nothing." "Oh are we going to know each other better." she said with a twinkle in her eye.""You can count on it." "I'd like nothing better." said Linda. When the wedding was over, Tom and Monica disappeared out the door to a waiting car, that the Marines had loaded with tin cans tied to the rear.

They clanged and clattered as they pulled away. Jim and Linda watched from the door and she reached for his hand. He held her hand firmly and then he put his arm around her. She looked at him and smiled. He escorted her to her quarters and they exchanged phone numbers and addresses. He told her he would call her soon. He said "I have something extremely important coming up this week." "I'll call you as soon as it's taken care of." She kissed him and told him "I'll wait for you call."

CHAPTER XX

When Jim met Alex, they just hugged and no words exchanged for what seemed a long time. Jim looked at his old friend and said "You must be the reincarnate of St. Anthony." Alex started to cry. Tears ran down his cheek. He was so happy that he was able to do something for his friend. "They're coming tomorrow." said Jim. "I do so want to meet them too."Alex said through his tears. Alex asked Jim to tell him all about his adventures in Afghanistan. They sat down and Jim told the story about the "phony" Bin Laden and the capture of the "tunnel" and the ultimate chase on horseback. "Sounds like a western movie." said Alex. "I got a chance to meet some wonderful people, like Tom Bragg." "I was best man at his wedding." "Any nice looking girls at the wedding?" "I'll tell you about that later. Tell me about this new program." "You know the Facial Recognition. It sounds very interesting." Alex proceeded to tell Jim about the way it was used to find Brian Ferguson. When he told Jim about preventing the priest from giving him his last confession. Jim laughed. "St. Anthony, I'm surprised at you, denying a man his last request for salvation." Jim listened intently about how his wife died at her own hands and he became very upset. "I've got to find where they buried her." "She needs to be laid to rest properly." "Maybe the kids can help you find the place." said Alex. "Maybe, maybe." "But first I just want to see them and talk to them and see what kind of persons they've grown up to be." He met them at Islip MacArthur Airport with a limousine. They sat in the back of the car and drank champagne. They laughed and hugged and cried. The limousine took them directly to the Holiday Inn which was really just around the corner. "You rented a limousine for a two mile ride, Dad?" "Actually, he's a friend of mine and this trip was on the arm." "On the arm, what does that mean" said Jim's son. Ann chuckled. "It means he got it free, you jerk." They all laughed heartily at Jim's naivety.

Once the kids got settled in at the hotel and they had dinner, they all started to talk about the years that had passed and the terrible tragedy of the loss of their mother. Jim was a Forensic Investigator and he told his father that he had even worked on Flight 800 as an intern. He was there when they identified one of the victims solely on the hairs from an electric razor. "We matched the DNA from the little hairs in the razor with the DNA of one of the victims. It was amazing." Ann was studying to be a computer programmer. "Good god, It's like you were both meant to be part of my vocation. Jim told them a little bit about "Investicom" and they both listened with amazed looks on their faces. "You mean this computer can do all that you say." "It can do so much more. Because it is Top Secret, I can't even tell you some of it's capabilities. He asked them about their mother and where were they taken to when they were first abducted. Jim said " Dad, from what I remember, it was a small house in the woods. It was near a river, I think." Jim asked him if he could remember anything else that might identify the location. "No, that's all that I remember." "Wait, there was a video taken, by the kidnappers.""They used it to show to the McPherson family, when they were going to sell us for adoption." "Where is that Video now?" " It's at home in a trunk that had Mom's, I mean Mrs. McPherson's belongings that we saved when she checked into the Nursing Home.

"Is there anyone back in Windsor, who could get the video and send it to us." Jim thought for a moment. "There is a neighbor who we have known and trusted for years. She has the keys to the house and we could ask her to fetch it for us. I just have to give her a call. "Please make the call Jim" said his father." "Tomorrow we are going to meet Alex and have dinner with him. He is my partner and he is responsible for finding you. I call him St. Anthony."

The next day they all had lunch together at a nice Italian Restaurant called the Casa Rustica. Alex ordered the wine. They chatted and Alex raised his glass at lunch and said "Heerz tay uz, Whawz like uz" Which means in Celtic May the best you've ever seen be the worst you' ll ever see. "Why Alex where in the world did ever hear that one?" "I used to hang out with some cots, before I met you."

The kids loved him and when they all broke up and left, they gave him a big hug not before they told him about the tape that they hoped would come in the mail. Alex said "We'll get permission first, then we'll run it through "Investicom". This time they got permission to run the tape through the computer. It wasn't hard to do. William Colin used his influence and his argument was that "We need to do things for our agents that don't fall in the line of policy." The tape was run through the same program that was used to find Bin Laden. It identified the area as Windsor and in the background was the Windsor- Detroit Tunnel toll plaza.

Jim bought airline tickets for all of them and they flew to Detroit. From there they rented a car and drove to the area of the Windsor Tunnel. They drove up and down streets, looking for a house that had the tunnel in the background of the house. Finally, they found a house that looked like a match. Jim's son almost jumped out of the car. "This is it." The house was abandoned and in poor repair. The number on it read 111 Sin Lane. "How appropriate." he thought. It had an old" For Sale" sign on the lawn, which hadn't been cut in years. Jim went to the Wayne County Sheriff's Office and told them about the possibility of his wife having been buried in the back yard of 111 Sin Lane. They were very sympathetic. One of the Deputies, an old timer, remembered that there had been some strange characters living in that house and he was always a little suspicious. "But then they left one day and the house was taken over by the bank, but it was so run down, no one ever bought it." he said.

The Sheriff's Office came the next day with a back hoe and started to dig in and around the property. It was a small machine and could maneuver well in a small space. Jim watched for a while, but then he left. He didn't want to be there if they came up with a body. The Deputies would inform him at the local motel, when and if anything was found. He went back to the motel with the kids and they had dinner and waited. The back hoe had dug up about four or five holes when they came up with some bones that appeared human. There was some fabric from a dress also. The remains were taken to the Wayne County Morgue. Jim was informed of what had been found. He insisted on going to the Morgue alone, without the kids. When he got there, he was shown the fabric first and he knew right away that it was part of the dress that his wife was wearing when she was abducted. There was nothing else there that he could view that would help him to identify the body remains. The Medical Examiner asked him if he had any dental records and he said that the Dentist that they used still had an office in Long Island. He would inform him to furnish the records to the ME. He asked when the remains could be released for a proper burial and they told him that as soon as the dental records are obtained and a positive identification is made, he could make arrangements. He got on the telephone and called the Dentist and he got Dr. Vick.

"Dr. Vick, you remember me, Jim Feron.?"Then he told him why they needed the records. "I'll Fed Ex them out today."" And Jim, you have my deepest sympathy, I remember her as being a lovely lady."

The burial was a quiet one. Elizabeth was laid to rest with her whole family present. No one cried but there was a heavy feeling of remorse among all of them. After the funeral, they had a small but quiet dinner for all the family and friends at a local restaurant.

CHAPTER XXI

The kids had to go back to Windsor after the funeral to straighten up their affairs before they would come back to Long Island and live with their father. This had been decided before they found Elizabeth. The family would be reunited and with both of their vocations it would be no problem finding them a job. In addition, Jim had plans to incorporate their talents into the "Investicom" program.

Jim and Alex went back to work working on new programs all the time. "Investicom" was so advanced that they had to think about a new location. William Colin had plans to move the computer anyway. He wanted to move it to Washington, but they wanted to stay on Long Island. Jim decided that he would search for a location that would suit everyone.

There was a location in Central Islip, where the Psychiatric Hospital used to be. There were several unused buildings that could be renovated to house the project. Security fences could be installed and it would be an unobtrusive location, that people would not question. They would simply think it was a renewal of the Hospital. Jim suggested the location to Colin and he said that he would send some of his people there to look it over and get back to him with suggestions and recommendations. The recommendations were positive and work began on setting up a new location for the Computer laboratory for "Investicom". Jim and Alex were very happy with the plans that were proposed. The new project would take several months to complete. Jim and Alex were in the middle of a project one day when the phone rang and Alex answered it.

"Jim, it 's for you. It's Tom Bragg." Jim picked up the phone and heard this voice."Hey best man, I'm going to be in town with my wife and we want to meet you for dinner," "How about it, pal?" "You say were and when." said Jim. "Tomorrow, at La Grange Restaurant in West Islip." "Okay, what time?" "Six O'clock for cocktails and then dinner on me. No arguments."

"Okay?" "Okay, you son of a gun." Jim and Alex met Tom and his new bride at the bar and everyone hugged and kissed. Jim couldn't believe how radiant Monica looked.

"Hey, you never called my sister, Linda." "Why not?" "I would have but I've been very involved right now, I'll explain it to you." "I fully intend to call her though." They had dinner and after dinner drinks and then Tom got Jim aside and said "Jim, we have to have a quiet drink together alone." "I've got some business to attend to you with you." They all drove to the Holiday Inn except for Alex who excused himself. Monica, knowing that there was something her husband had to discuss with Jim also excused herself and went up to their room. Jim was curious as to what Tom was being so mysterious about. He was to learn shortly. They sat in a quiet lounge in the Hotel Bar and had a couple of B&B's.

Jim waited for Tom to talk. He sipped his B&B and then he spoke. "Jim, do you remember when we were in Afghanistan and we , I mean you discovered that secret room in the tunnel?" Jim nodded."Well remember there was some shredded documents that we sent to Washington and later on one of my officers asked what was in the shredded documents." "Yes, I remember and I have to admit I was very curious as to what was in the documents, but we were too busy at the time as I remember."

"I can tell you now about some of the information because I need your contacts in the New York Police Department for a very important assignment. So important that it could effect New York City almost if not more so than the World Trade Center attack." He said this with the most stern, serious look that he actually frightened Jim. "Tom, I'll do anything I can, You know that." "Jim what I'm about to tell you can never be repeated to a living soul." "The second part of what I'm about to tell you could effect our country and the city of New York and could kill an awful lot of New Yorkers." Jim looked into his eyes and he could tell that this was something that the country and city should be deeply concerned with.

"The first thing I will tell you is about material that was analyzed from the shredded documents we took out of the tunnel." "It told of a plan whereby two agents from Al- Qu'aida were to buy a boat. Something like a Boston Whaler type fishing boat. One of the men on the boat had been practicing shooting some captured Russian made missiles called the SA18 or the Russian name for them was "Igla". It has a range of 15,000 feet. The boat was to wait offshore in the Moriches and wait for a radio transmission." "The message would be coded and would indicate that an airplane had left Kennedy and was in the area." " The one man who was now an expert at firing the "Igla" would attempt the shot. It would be a shoulder fired missile." "We now believe that based on this information and all of the witnesses that said they saw a streak of smoke rising toward the aircraft, that it indeed was shot down by Al Qu'aida." "Once the missile was fired and the hit accomplished the two men in the boat would take Cyanide tablets and scuttle the boat."

"We have recovered parts of the boat and traced it's purchase to a known member of Bin Laden's group." "He went under the name of Omar Mateen." "We have traced him to locations in Philadelphia, Atlanta and Boston." "We think that he may be in New York right now.""We want your "Investicom" to try to screen telephone calls throughout the city.""Can such a thing be done?" Jim replied "We can set up a program which intercepts microwave transmissions emitted from telephones and homes in on key words like bomb or gas or some of the nicknames used by Bin Laden like "The Prince, the Director, Emir, Abu, and some of his other aliases." "We can set up a glossary of terms that the computer will home in on and possibly locate your friend Mr. Mateen."

CHAPTER XXII

The program used by "Investicom" to intercept telephonic communications was similar to one suspected to be used by the Soviets during the Cold War. They allegedly had a super technological setup at their embassy in Glen Cove, which had the capability to home in on keywords from our defense plants such as Grumman and Fairchild. A word like "test flight" or "test pilot" would send signals to their computer and from then on the conversations from that source would be intercepted. Some times the terms came from non technical sources. Once this was determined the interception ceased.

"Investicom" had a huge task. You can imagine the amount of telephone traffic coming out of New York City and you can also imagine how many times persons of a non-technical background or suspicious background would talk about Bin Laden and the Al-Qu'aida, simply because they were the topics of the day. How many conversations were as a result of a current news cast or radio broadcast. "Investicom" clicked and clattered and lights flashed off and on signaling that the computer had picked up a suspicious word or phrase. This operation went on for weeks without a concrete result. Both Jim and Alex and Tom Bragg were beginning to get discouraged that "Investicom" would not be able to find active terrorists in the New York area in time to prevent some sort of attack Then a series of calls using key words came in from three separate sources. The big computer determined also that the calls were exchanging communications. So now "Investicom" had three separate sources that were suspect. Ex Parte Orders (Wiretap permission) were obtained from a Federal Judge and wiretaps were initiated on the locations.

"Did you ever work a wiretap Tom." said Jim. "No, that's what we've got you for.""Okay, we'll work it together." "We'll need a crew for surveillance."

"The NYPD and the FBI are supplying their best men for that." They set up the wiretap in the basement of a school which was near the target. The target being a flat on the east side of Manhattan on 21st Street. Jim had to learn all the new technology of wiretapping. "This is so much more advanced than the equipment we used to use." he said. "No more Penn Registers." Now the phone number on the incoming call appeared instantly on a device similar to the one on a telephone."The calls were not "minimized" as was necessary in State Wiretaps. This was a different story. All of the conversations were pertinent. They could have code words and phrases that would have to be deciphered. In addition they had to have someone sit on the tap with them who understood Arabic and the many languages of the Afghans.

Tom introduced a new member of the wiretap. "This is Sea Unis. He is an Egyptian-American. He is with the Bureau and he is a linguistic expert. We'll need him in case we run up against some languages we don't know. "

"You mean like anything besides English." said Jim.

"Yeah, I didn't fare to well in school with languages either." said Tom." "Glad to know you Sea." said Jim

"Ever work a wiretap?" "No." "What languages are you familiar with?" "I can speak Arabic, Pashto Northern, Pashto Southern, Pahlavani, Parachi, Kamviri, Domari, Savi, ..." "Okay, Okay, you'll do fine." "I can also speak French, Spanish, German, Italian and Russian.""How can you remember all these languages." "I don't really know, all I know is I do."

During the first week of the wiretap, Sea was called on to interpret several conversations in Pashto. They were seemingly harmless conversations. Mostly they were about horse races and baseball. It seems our Afghani suspects had a love for American horse racing and baseball. The conversations continued and both Jim and Tom started to become suspicious. "Do you think it is some kind of a code." said Tom.

"Could be."

The transcripts were forwarded to Washington to an Encryption Decoding section. Jim kept reading the transcripts over and over. The latest conversation seemed a little more urgent from the tone of the voices. Of course it was in Pashto and had to be interpreted by Sea before they could even try to decipher it. Sea gave Jim a typed transcript of the latest conversation which went "Do you know the results of last nights games between Boston and the Orioles and LA and San Francisco." "Yes, Boston and LA both won. You can pick up your winnings." "Do you have any tips on the races at Belmont today?""Yes, take the horse that jockey Samuels rides in the first race. In the second race take the number2 to Win and number 1 to place position. Take the number 2 horse in the third to Win. In the fourth race number 1 and he stressed the word "Win" "In the fifth race take the number 1 horse again to Win." But this time there was no emphasis on the word "Win". "In the last race take the two and the five to Win You must make these bets. Get to the track early because you must get the bets down, understand."

Jim played a little game of his own with the transcripts. Tom asked him "What are you doing?" "I don't know. It's like a game of Wheel of Fortune."

"That's it, maybe the letters mean something." He continued using combinations and then it came clear to him. Boston and LA. Could that be Bin Laden? "BLA"

"A message from Bin Laden. "What about the horse races.""Samuels is the jockey in the first race. Letter S. The second race I have number 2 to win and number 1 to place. 21. That would be a U. The third race post position 2. That would be the letter B.""The fourth race post position 1 another A.""The fifth race post position 1 again, another A that would be A Then in the last race we take the 2 and the five, 25 or the letter Y. Now we have SUBAAY.""What the hell is that?" "Wait."" In the fourth race he stressed the word"Win". "Let's take a W for that " Now we have SUBWAY." "I think you've hit on something Jim" said Tom.

"They are going to do something to the subway system.

Maybe something similar to what happened in Tokyo. The surveillance teams were alerted and the subject of the wiretap Mr. Omar Mateen, who was now going under the name of Omar Farzi was discreetly followed to two locations. A house in East Elmhurst, Queens near LaGuardia Airport and another in Astoria near the TriBoro Bridge.

Both homes were kept under constant surveillance. There were several occupants in both houses as determined by the comings and goings. Photographic surveillance and another Ex Parte order for wiretaps were obtained.

There was one house which had not been known of which was the home of a Banker. He was the President of the National Life Bank of Pakistan and from the conversations he was friendly to the group. They did all of their banking with the National Bank and while inside they were observed sitting down with bank members until they were ushered into an inside room which read Private.

It was decided that a search warrant would be obtained for the Bank. But the search would be performed at night and without any previous notice to the subjects of the warrant. This was unusual but they could not compromise the investigation by letting anyone know that they were watching and listening to them.

The search was done at Midnight. This they believed was the safest hour. The Midnight shift of the local Police Precinct would not be out on patrol yet. The 4 to 12 shift would be on their way in to sign out for the evening. It was arranged as a further safeguard to have the FBI give a little lecture to the Midnight tour about Terrorism. This was done on all three shifts so as not make anything look suspicious.

The lecture would last about a half hour. The precinct was still able to send units out should an emergency arise. This would give the "intruders" a little more time to disable the alarms and start their search. Jim and Tom would play "chickie" outside the bank in case any one approached the bank. They were in constant touch by radio with the men inside.

CHAPTER XXIII

The team entering the bank had to disable the alarm system and also the local Precinct could not be told what was going on. This presented quite a problem. An expert team was assembled to disable the Central Station Alarm System which would alert the local Police Precinct. Once the Alarm system was disabled, the search could begin. The search would have be so discreet as to not reveal that anyone had been there. Any documents considered valuable would have to be copied. Everything would have to be photographed. No trace of entry could be left to the watchful eyes of the enemy.

They were in the area of the bank at 11:45 PM. The Alarm team parked their cars in a lot that had some small stores across the street from the bank. It was just two of them. They walked across the street and went right to the big glass door. There was hardly any traffic. Just an occasional car. They made sure that they crossed the street when their wasn't any traffic in sight. The team disabled the alarm in minutes. They were in. "Boy, they're good." said Jim. "Yeah, real professionals" Now the search team went across. Five agents and NYPD Detectives made up this team. They went in past one of the alarm team who opened the door for them.

It was 12:45PM and the Midnight shift had heard their lecture and were ready to perform their patrol duties. "Lets go down Center Street, there's an all night Diner down there and we can get ourselves some coffee and a roll."

"How about it?" said the Patrolman. His partner nodded.

"Sounds good to me."

They drove down Center Street and were a block away from the bank when they pulled into the curb. Jim and Tom both saw them at the same time."What's he doing?" said Jim. "Get out of there, You'll screw everything up." The radio car had stopped because one of the Patrolmen, the driver was looking for his wallet. "It's okay." he said to his partner. "I thought I left my money back in my locker." "Oh sure, I know that trick, just so you don't have to buy." "Is it my turn again."

"Never mind I"ll buy. It won't break me.""You get it next time and they pulled away from the curb passed the bank and down Center Street to the Diner. "Whoosh" said Jim. Inside the bank, the team searched the room marked "Private," It was locked and they picked the lock. They had on night vision glasses so no lights needed to be used. There was a window and some light came in from a street light. They looked in the desk drawers and opened a file cabinet. There didn't seem to be any suspicious documents anywhere. There was a picture on a wall behind the desk and one of the men found that it had a hinge and opened like a door. Behind it was a safe. One of the men was a safe man. He could open any safe that was ever made. He used his expertise to moonlight for locksmiths. Whenever a locksmith got a call from someone who had a relative with a safe and no one knew the combination, he got a call. He was better than "Raffles" or even "The Phantom" from the "Pink Panther".

The safe cracker, Tony Sara, went to work. First Left on the combination wheel, then right and then left again. Finally there was a little click and he turned the handle and the safe was open. What they found was treasure or for the want of a better name it was as Tom Bragg called it "The plan from Hell.

The "Plan from Hell" as it was now named was taken back to Police Headquarters where it would be analyzed and plans formulated to defense against it.

The Plan was for five Terrorists to enter five different subway stations. Each of them was armed with a canister of Sarin, a nerve gas. The canisters would be punctured inside of the subway cars. This was a plan similar to the one used in the Tokyo subway lines. One train was on the line headed downtown toward Wall Street. The other was scheduled to stop at 42nd Street. The third was headed for 59th Street and the fifth would go to 72nd Street. All of these stops during the rush hour had thousands of people riding in the subway cars.

The plan was to photograph all of the persons in the houses, which was done from the window of homes across the street from the houses. All of the men in the houses were photographed and the photos were cataloged as to location.

This is where "Investicom's" Facial Recognition would be put into operation. Cameras were set up at all of the key subway stations. As soon as someone passed through the toll turn style, his or her picture was taken and immediately compared to the photos gathered through the surveillance. The wiretap received calls about the races again. This time the conversation interpreted into English went like this. In the first race take the number five horse. In the second race take the two to win and the four to place. Third race the number five again. The fourth race take number three. In the fifth race the numbers two and one. Use your own judgment on the rest. Jim figured them out. First race E, second race X. third E again. Fourth is C and the fifth race U. EXECU. "Execute" "That's what it means." "Tom, lets roll." "Let's roll Jim" said Tom.

The teams were set up at the subway entrances with the cameras in place. Now all they could do was wait for them to EXECUTE. There would be no surveillance because of the chance of being "made." They would rely solely on "Investicom" and the Facial Recognition Program.

The teams were in place for the early rush hour. At the first subway station, a large afro-american New York City Police Officer named Evan Hughes was stationed at the turn style with a microphone placed in his ear. He would be alerted once a recognition was made of one of the terrorists. It was 7:54 AM when the first terrorist entered the subway station with trains to Wall Street. The subway was crowded. As he passed through the turn style, Evan Hughes was alerted .

Hughes had once had a tryout with the New York Giants as a Line Backer. He played for Nebraska and was a fifth round draft pick. He just never made the pros. He spotted his target. As the man passed through the turn style he was taken to the ground like a Linebacker on a Quarterback blitz. He was blind sided and crunched to the ground. So much for Terrorist #1.

The second man was also passing through the turn style when he was identified. He got to the staircase which would take him to a lower platform, but that's as far as he got when a young lady walked in front of him and asked him if the train downstairs would take her to Times Square. He brushed past her, but she delayed him just long enough for two officers to bring him to the ground. He yelled

"Help, I am being robbed." and some people approached but the female pulled out her shield and said "Police, get back." Terrorist #2 was arrested.

Terrorists number three , four and five were taken in like fashion. All having been identified by Facial Recognition and stopped before they could get to the subway trains.

Jim and Tom, who were at Police Headquarters with some big Police brass and Supervising FBI agents got the word of the success of the operation. They all stood up and cheered. One of the Chiefs went over to a small refrigerator which was in the room and took out a bottle of Champagne. Everyone had a glass and toasted their success. "Here's to our country and our flag and the best things they stand for." said the Chief. "Here, here." all said.

CHAPTER XXIV

Tom Bragg wanted Jim to come home with him. He and Monica had settled in a house in Fairfax, Virginia. "Come on and have a visit." "Monica's sister is going to be there. We can go out and make it a foursome."

"What do you say?"

Jim wanted to very badly so he said he would after he went back to the Lab and saw that everything was working okay. He knew Alex would insist that he go. After he met with Alex and had called the kids in Windsor, he packed his bags for a weeks trip to Virginia. He was looking forward to seeing Monica's sister Linda again. He had a wonderful week in Virginia with Monica, Tom and Linda. They went to Williamsburg and had lunch in one of the old time pubs there.

They had dinner in an Irish style pub in Fairfax called "The Irish Coffee Pub". Jim remarked that there was an "Irish Coffee Pub" on Long Island in East Islip.They all sang "The Irish Soldier Boy" and "Danny Boy" and a host of other Irish favorites. All in all, Jim had a wonderful time. One night, Tom and Monica snuck away from them and left him alone with Linda. They had it all planned. He had a night cap with her and they laughed and drank their Drambuies and Sambucas. She was so much fun, he thought. Then the week was over and it came time for him to leave. They had dinner the last night together and then again he was alone with Linda as Tom and Monica said their goodbyes. They would not see him in the morning when he left. "Please keep in touch." said Monica. "Tom, loves you like a brother." "Me too." said Jim and they hugged and kissed and Tom and Monica left the restaurant.

Now he was alone again with Linda. He didn't know what to say.

He liked her very much and it was obvious that she liked him too. "Linda, I want to see you again. I have two children and I need to get to know them again." "I know."she said. "Do you think you could come up to Long Island for Thanksgiving which is only two months away?" "We could have a nice dinner, I mean an old style Thanksgiving Dinner at my house and you could meet my family." "I'd love to." she said. He escorted her to her car, where they kissed and said goodbye.

Jim arrived back at the lab and Alex who hardly moved as he walked in the door. Well, I hope I'm not disturbing you, Mr. Lermindov." Alex was engrossed in something and he just grunted "Hi, how are you, I'll be with you in a minute. Jim" "We have a new project and you're going to love it." "Mr. Colin called me yesterday and I've been working on it since then."

"Is it as big as the Afghan thing?" "Maybe bigger." said Alex. "We would work with the agency."

CHAPTER XXV

"Have you ever heard of USAMRIID?" asked Alex. "No, what does it stand for?" "It stands for the U. S. Army Medical Research Institute of Infectious Diseases." "They conduct research to develop strategies, products, and procedures and training for medical defense against biological warfare threats and infectious diseases. They are the lead medical research laboratory for the U.S.Biological Defense Research Program.

" "They have a staff of over four hundred physicians, vets, pathologists, chemists. Biologists and pharmacologists. "

One of their primary studies involves improved vaccines for Anthrax, Venezuelan equine encephalitis, plague and botulism and new vaccines for toxins such a staphylococcal entero toxins and ricin."

"One of their chemists has been unaccounted for since before the weekend. He said something to one of the staff about going away for the weekend and he didn't come back to work on Monday."" They sent some people to his home and his car is in the driveway and the house was all locked up with no one inside. They gained entry and everything was neat and tidy. Some clothes were missing from the closet and it looks like a suitcase from a set is gone. He has two brothers, one dead and another brother who is married but he never told him that he was going away or where. The neighbors haven't seen anything."

"At least they didn't see him leave from the house." "One neighbor said she heard a car come down her block sometime about 2:00 A.M. And turn around near his house, but she couldn't see if anyone got out or got in. The car left after only stopping for five minutes."

"What's so important about this guy?" said Jim. "He's in charge of a Top Secret Project which is involved in the immunization against Anthrax and some other toxins that the government suspects are in the hands of Sadam Hussein."

"I see." said Jim.

A few days later a special courier arrived at the laboratory with some additional information on the missing chemist, whose name was Alfred Carter. The file which included his PSQ (Personnel Security Questionnaire) showed that he was due to be re-investigated. His last "bring up" as they called it was done five years ago and because the work he was pursuing was so sensitive he would have to undergo a Polygraph Examination. Just before the scheduled "Poly" he disappeared.

"I guess this might indicate that he was afraid of the Polygraph test." said Jim. A further examination of his file showed that he had a brother who was a fighter pilot and fought in Vietnam. His brother, George was shot down in 1969 and there were some reports of his capture, but it was never confirmed and he was listed as Missing In Action – presumed dead.

Inside the report was an envelope which read "Sensitive Material". Jim opened the envelope and there was a report about George Carter. The report read that reports coming out of North Vietnam from Intelligence sources indicate that a pilot who was shot down on the date that George Carter went missing was taken prisoner and taken to a secret location under the supervision of the Viet Cong. This location according to sources was used by the VC to proselytize captured Americans. The theory of proselytization being that captured prisoners were brainwashed to where they could be released back to the United States to contribute to the anti-war movement.

Early in the war before 1968, North Vietnamese military and civilian personnel were hostile to U.S. Military personnel and often killed those who were captured. In 1969, a report compiled indicated that a report issued by the North Vietnamese Government stipulated that captured U.S, military and civilian personnel were to be kept alive for anticipated exchange and compensation. Special attention was to be paid to Americans who made specific achievements or came from wealthy families or had relatives in sensitive positions with the government. A special cadre was formed to accomplish the conversion of prisoners to cooperate.

Upon being captured, each American POW was required to complete a standard questionnaire. The purpose of the questionnaire was to collect information that could be used for the overall goals and mission of "promoting the antiwar movement". The cadre were interested in personal information from POW's concerning relatives, including their mailing addresses in the United States. Such information was obtained in an attempt to gain the support of the individual POW, his family and friends. And the American public. By using statements made by POW's, by "brainwashing" them the cadre hoped to spread dissension and anti war sentiment in the United States.

"This is very interesting." said Jim.

The investigation for the missing Chemist Alfred Carter. Toll records of his home phone and cell phone were obtained from the

Telephone Company. His bank records were scrutinized. Photos from the ATM machine at his bank were looked over. Some information started to develop. Carter's home telephone toll records and records of incoming and outgoing phone calls indicated a number of calls coming to his home from telephone booths located in various parts of Manhattan. Of course there was no way of knowing who had made these calls. They were made in drug stores, on the sidewalk, in restaurants and there was no pattern to the locations where they were made from.

The cell phone calls picked up something strange. Two calls outside of the Iraqi Embassy in Washington, D.C.A check of his financial records showed an ATM withdrawal on the Friday that he left work. The camera of that ATM was checked for the date and time of the withdrawal and it showed Carter at the machine with a man who looked like he was Asiatic standing just behind him.

The next report received out of Washington was that surveillance of the Iraq Embassy showed a limousine pull up at the gate and two men enter. One of them was Alfred Carter. The United States Department of State sent a message to the Iraq Diplomat telling him that the United States Government demanded the release of one of it's citizens from the Iraqi Embassy immediately. The return message stated that the Department of State was mistaken because the embassy did not house any American citizens.

"They've got him in there and they will not release him." Colin said to Jim and Alex over the telephone.

"What's our next step?" said Jim. "We wait" Colin replied. Jim was flown to Washington along with Alex. They were summoned to William Colin's office. As they entered the conference room. Colin greeted them and said "I've got someone here you'll be glad to see."

Tom Bragg entered the room. "I thought I got rid of you for a while." "Nah, a bad penny always turns up."

"We've devised a plan which Jim Feron has contributed to." "Since the Iraqis have decided to play hard ball, we will too." "We are going to knock out their phones first. It will unfortunately "be a line that went down from wear." "Then we'll wait for them to complain to the Telephone Company."

"We are going to attempt to bug the Embassy." "Jim has some contacts from NYPD Intelligence, Technical Services Section who are experts at putting bugs in right under the noses of our friends. The telephone lines were cut the next day and then they waited for the Embassy Officials to call the Telephone Company Repair. But, they didn't call. Two days went by and they didn't call. "They're making their calls from cell phones, but eventually that will be too inconvenient and they'll call." said Colin.

They had their usual early morning briefing in Colin's conference room. A secretary came in with a plate full of donuts. Everyone had their coffee and donuts when the phone rang in the conference room. The phone calls were screened so that only very important calls were let through.

"They called the phone company. Now the ball is in our court." Jim's friends from Intelligence drove their "Telephone Company" truck up to the front gate of the embassy. They were let inside and they went to work. They were watched very closely by a couple of the embassy staff.

They put the bug in the earpieces of the telephones. Outside, they had men waiting until the operation was completed then they spliced the wires back and the telephone service was restored. The bugs were in place and now they set up their "plant" for listening to the conversations.

Their old friend Sea Unis was used again to interpret. It turned out that he wasn't really needed because the first good conversation was in English.

"It's Carter" said Bragg. It sounds like an interrogation." That's what it was. They were asking him all sorts of questions about his duties and the Project that he was working on. It was an intense question and answer session and it was obvious that he was under a lot of stress from the tone of his voice. After several hours the interrogation ended and the interrogators and Carter left the room. There were no more conversations worth listening to until the next day when they started again, only this time there were different interrogators.

There was now some new foreign language involved and Sea said "That's not a language that I am familiar with. I believe that it is either Korean or a Northern Chinese dialect." This forced the team to obtain another interpreter. They could only listen to conversations and record them until they could get someone to interpret them for them. The tape was sent to a unit run by the CIA that had language experts. They were to be interpreted and transcribed.

CHAPTER XXVI

The new conversations turned out to be Korean. It was determined that it was a North Korean Staff Officer who was talking. Now it became clear. They had Alfred's brother, George. He had been cooperating with the North Vietnamese since a year after his capture. Another conversation was interpreted as Vietnamese. In between using their own languages they spoke French. They were trying to get Alfred Carter to give them the formula for the antidote to Anthrax. They were cooperating fully with the Iraqi government. It would be equally beneficial to both of their governments. He was resisting them, but they made it quite clear that they had his brother and his brother wanted him to cooperate. They would arrange it that he could speak to his brother via video e-mail. He said "I would like to see and speak to my brother." "It will be done." said one of the Iraqi diplomats." The next day, a conversation was intercepted which had Alfred Carter and his brother speaking for the first time in over thirty years. Alfred asked him all sorts of questions."How are you?" "Did they mistreat you?" "No, they have treated me fine." said George."But you have to give them what they want. They have unspeakable ways of torturing people and they have promised me that I will suffer them all." "I'll give them what they want, but will they release you if I do?" "I don't know, I don't know if we can trust them." A voice interrupted the conversation between the two brothers. "You can rest assured that if you cooperate we will send you brother home to you." Alfred Carter's voice shook as he said " Please send him home. I'll do what you want."

A decision had to be made about Alfred Carter and it had to be made by William Colin and his superiors. Jim and Tom Bragg continued to listen to the "bug" but there were no more interrogations involving Carter.

Even as they waited it could turn out to be too late for them to stop Carter from supplying information about the antidote to Anthrax. The decision came from the highest possible source. There would be no asking the UN to step in. It had to be done by the United States and their closest ally which was Great Britain. Any procrastinating could prove to be disastrous.

It was the middle of summer and in Washington the temperatures could get up well over a 100 as everyone knew. Now they would shut off the electricity or it would go off accidentally .This made the embassy very warm, but not uninhabitable. The next step was to set up large heat deflectors from trucks parked outside the embassy. They would project warm air just as would be used in a private home to help heat the house. Only they were much larger and much more powerful.

The temperatures inside of the embassy would reach a mark of over 110 degrees. Once the procedure started, the phones inside started to hum. Calls were made to the local Gas and Electric companies, however they were told that there was a problem and the Gas and Electric company was working on it and it would take time. The people inside started to collapse from the heat and then panic set in and they started to run out of the building. As they attempted to escape the heat they were met by so called Doctors and Nurses with waiting ambulances which spirited them away to a "hospital" They never questioned the validity of the doctors or nurses because they were so anxious to get out of the building. Eventually everyone was out of the building except no Alfred Carter. At this point, the local fire department was sent in to "save" any one trapped inside the building. They got Alfred Carter out. They had to search the building and they eventually found him in a basement apartment which was tantamount to being a cell. Once they got him out, they took him to a private hospital, where he was treated and debriefed by members of Colin's staff. He was debriefed and he told the members of Colin's staff that he had not yet given enough information to the Iraqis for them to produce an antidote to Anthrax. He was very concerned though that they would retaliate against his brother, George.

He was shown secret information about his brother, George. His brother initially had cooperated with the North Vietnamese, however, a CIA operative working in a Hanoi hospital confirmed that George Carter died from pneumonia in 1970. He even managed to smuggle out a photo of him in the morgue. The North Vietnamese Government kept his death a secret. They hoped to use the fact that he was being held a prisoner to some advantage. That advantage arose when they were approached by the Iraqis, who had information that George Carter's brother was a scientist working on the antidote to Anthrax.

"You have to believe us, Alfred, your brother is dead." "But I spoke to him on video e-mail" "That was an imposter." said William Colin.

Information was given out to the press that there was a power failure at the Iraqi Embassy and all of the diplomats were rescued safely except for one man, who could not be identified and died from a heart attack from the exposure to the extreme heat. (Alfred Carter) but his name was not released. This was a ploy.

CHAPTER XXVII

Jim got a telephone call from Tom Bragg. Tom told him that he and his wife would be coming to New York. "Jim, we want to be with you and your family for the holiday. Do you think you could put us up for Thanksgiving?" "Are you kidding, We'd love to have you."

"It would be so great to have you. What about Monica's sister Linda?"

"Will she be coming with you?" "Jim, Linda will not be coming. She is going to call you tonight." "Is anything wrong?" said Jim. "She'll call you tonight." Tom emphasized. From his tone, Jim knew there was some sort of problem with Linda coming. He decided to wait for her call.

"Okay, pal, we'll have a huge turkey and you'll have a chance to meet my kids."

"It sounds wonderful, Jim, see ya."

Jim got the call from Linda that evening.

"Hi" she said. "You're not coming are you?" Jim asked. "No, I really can't. Jim I have to tell you something. I met this guy. He's an officer in the Navy and I really don't know what happened. I just fell madly for him. It happened so suddenly, I can't explain it. I'm sorry." Jim hesitated for amoment and then he spoke "Linda, I can't say what might have happened between us, if we would have eventually become more than friends. I just want to say that I liked you very much. I want to wish you and your fella the very best and I want you to know that I'll always be your friend."

"Thank you Jim and God Bless You."Jim hung up the phone and he sat thinking of what might have been with Linda. She was a lovely girl but it was not meant to be, he thought. He decided to call his kids and get ready for Thanksgiving.

The dinner was a very happy affair. They had two turkeys, fully stuffed with sausage stuffing. Candied Yams, mashed potatoes, green beans, salad, all adorned the table. Jim got all the food from a local caterer that specialized Thanksgiving dinners. A Magnum of Champagne was opened and squirted all over everyone. The all laughed and ducked from the spray. Jim got up and gave a toast. "Here's health to all those we love, here's health to all those that love us. Here's health to all those that love them, that love those, that love them, that love us." "I remember that one from our wedding." said Tom Bragg. "I loved it then and I love it now.

The dinner ended with everyone stuffed with turkey. After an "after dinner aperitif everyone sat in easy chairs and talked about good times. There would be no unhappy conversations allowed. Tom and his wife and Jim's kids became very good friends. Jim just sat and enjoyed the company. After two or three hours, Jim's daughter said "Hey how about a turkey sandwich.?" It was like they hadn't eaten at all. They all had a turkey sandwich and a glass of beer. When they were all too tired to move, Tom and his wife Monica excused themselves and went up to the guest room that was prepared for them. John and Elizabeth excused themselves also. They kissed their father and went to bed. Jim sat in the living room in a nice soft easy chair. He sipped a Drambuie and reflected about the day. He thought about his wife, and Anne and Linda. He fell asleep and the glass fell from his hand. After a while he got up and went to bed.

CHAPTER XXVIII

For the next six months, Jim arranged with Colin to train his son and daughter in the operation of "Investicom". Of course they had to go through the lengthy procedure of a Background Investigation. This took six weeks. After they had passed through the process, Jim started with the training. He was proud that they both took to the training like ducks to water. He was very happy that he would be able to pass the torch on to members of his family.

He was not the only one thrilled to have the Ferons involved in the research. Alex took to them like a Grand parent. He was loving and kind and extremely helpful in the training. He relished it. They became like members of his family. He never felt such gratification. John got so involved with 'Investicom" that he started to develop a spin off of the Facial Recognition program. He was very excited as he explained to his father the new aspect of the program.

"It does the same thing only with objects, like cars, boats, all kinds of inanimate objects." "Think of what we can do to identify stolen cars that have had their VIN numbers changed. The computer would be able to recognize that there was a change made." "It would identify a boat that has been repainted to disguise it or had it's registration number changed on the hull." It has all sorts of possibilities." "It sounds great," said Jim. "Keep at it."

After six months, Alex and Jim decided that both John and Elizabeth could now be left alone to operate the computer. Both Jim and Alex had decided to take a vacation. Jim would go to England and visit Anne's sister, Pam and Alex had planned to take a cruise. "I've never been on one. Maybe I'll meet a rich widow and you'll lose a partner." he joked. "That'll be the day."said Jim. They parted. Going their separate ways. John and Elizabeth could always contact them should an emergency arise, but Jim and Alex had such confidence in their trainees that they were not the least bit concerned. Jim caught a plane for England the day after he saw Alex off on his Caribbean Cruise. Alex got on board the Carioca II and immediately found his cabin and then went to the lobby bar, which was open. He had himself a frozen Margarita and sat and watched television It was 2:00 P.M. And the ship was not due to sail until 4:00 P.M. He indulged himself, having four Margaritas. There was plenty of time before dinner. He was on the early seating, which was at 5:45 P.M. Meanwhile Jim's plane was over the Atlantic and still a few hours from the airport in London. He read a magazine, had a Martini and then dozed off.

When he landed, he immediately called his old friend Hector Thomson. They would have dinner and few drinks together. They hugged as they met in the dining room of the Lion Arms Pub in Soho, London. "How've you been, Jim?" said Hector. "Not bad and you?" "Good" said Jim They sat down and had a couple of pints together before dinner. "I'm going up to Scotland to see Anne's sister, Pam.""You still haven't gotten over her death, have you?" "I guess not." said Jim.

"Jim, I have to tell you about the crash. I hope it won't upset you." "Go ahead,"said Jim. "There was nothing to identify her except a credit card with some blood on it." It was her credit card of course, There was nothing, but she couldn't have suffered because when the taxi she was in it the gas truck, it exploded and there was nothing, nothing."

"I hope that this doesn't upset you, but you can at least rest assured that she died instantly." "Thanks, Hector" "I'm glad that it was over quickly." They changed the subject and had a pleasant dinner and a couple of drinks.

"Going up to Edinburgh to see Pam are you?" "She's a lovely girl, looks a little like Anne." "Yeah I met her at the funeral." "Oh, that's right, I forgot."

"Hey come back down here and this time we'll tie one on, okay?" "You got it." said Jim. Jim had his visit with Pam Fulton and met her fiancee, Frank, a very friendly fellow who worked in a local pub. They had dinner and drinks and found that they all had a lot in common. Pam told him things about Anne that he never knew and he was grateful. It was like she was there herself telling him about her likes and dislikes, hobbies, movies she liked, books she read, and so on. Jim left with a sincere feeling of calm. He asked Pam and her boy friend to come and visit him and his family and they said they had been planning a visit to the United States anyway. They were thrilled at the thought of visiting him and his kids.

Jim returned to London and his return visit with Hector and then made his plans to return to the United States. His last night in London, he and Hector did "tie one on" as they said and they laughed and hugged and joked with some single ladies atthe bar. Jim finally excused himself and said his goodbyes to Hector and went to bed.

His bags were already packed so all he had to do was get up at 5:00 A.M. It was already 3:00 A.M. So he would not get much sleep. He told the desk to make sure that they woke him so he could make his "red eye " flight. All he would get would be a slight doze until they called. So he didn't undress. He just sat in an easy chair and closed his eyes. He went to sleep almost immediately and he dreamed. Again he had his same recurring dream about Elizabeth. She was so beautiful and she was smiling.

"Elizabeth, why did you leave me?" "I didn't want to honey, but you have the children with you now and I am so happy." "Jim, I have to tell you about Anne, she isn't dead."

"What are you saying sweetheart?" He awoke in a sweat as the phone rang. "Mr. Feron, it's the desk, you asked us to call you."

"Thank you, I'll be right down."" Please call a taxi for me to take me to the airport."

"We'll take care of that for you sir. Have a pleasant trip and come back again." We'll have your bill all ready for you when you come down." Jim boarded his plane and it was no time before he went back to sleep again. There was no dream this time. At least none that he remembered when he awoke. The stewardess woke him with a cup of coffee.

"Would you like a little breakfast, sir." "We have some scrambled eggs and ham and toast." "Sounds great." said Jim and he stretched and stood up in the aisle. He looked out of the port window and he could see the ocean and the sun coming up through the clouds. "I wonder how St. Anthony is making out on his cruise." he thought. His plane circled and came into Kennedy and it touched down like a whisper. He had gone to the bathroom and washed his face and now he was ready to go back to work.

CHAPTER XXIX

Alex was having a grand time. He sat with some very interesting people from Texas. They were retired ranch owners and very friendly. After dinner he would go to the casino and play the quarter slot machines. He won the first night about seventy dollars, but he gave it all back the following evening. He was having fun. The first port of call was Key West. He got off the ship and went sightseeing. He happened to notice some of the crew getting off also. They went off down the street laughing and joking. He saw them disappear near a row of bars. Alex strolled down the street and walked into Sloppy Joe's, where he had a drink and bought a tee shirt with Ernest Hemingway's picture on it.

"Jim will like this." he thought. The ship was in port until 8:00 P.M. The sun set around 7:30 PM so it was dark when the stragglers got back to the ship. The crew went on without much ado. They walked past the passengers who went through he usual check point security. Alex was on board early enough to attend the late seating for dinner. The gangway crew lifted the gang plank and the ship slipped easily out of the harbor for it's next destination, which was the Turks and Caicos Islands. Dinner was long over and Alex had lost his usual

50 dollars on the slots. He had a B&B in the Casino Lounge and then went to his cabin.

He was awakened by a sound outside of his cabin. He heard some voices and a lot of scuffling. It sounded like a dispute or a fight. He rolled over and decided it was a honeymoon couple who were not getting along. Early the next morning, he woke up to a ringing bell used for the lifeboat drill. A voice came over the loudspeaker requesting that all passengers put on their life preservers and proceed to their assigned boat stations. The stewards would be at their posts directing all of the passengers down the stairs to the assigned decks. Alex got up rather slowly and started to get dressed.

"Damn stupid lifeboat drills." he muttered and just threw on a pair of shorts and a tee shirt. "What time is it." he said to himself. He looked at the clock in the stateroom and it read 6:00 A.M.

"What an ungodly hour to stage a drill." he complained.

As he gathered up his life jacket and put it around his neck he opened the cabin door and saw people walking along the aisles headed for the stairwells. There were female and male stewards stationed in the hallways. Somehow, Alex thought to himself "They don't look very happy either, about this drill." But there was more than just a look of annoyance on their faces. They had a look of fear also. Alex got an uneasy feeling, that maybe this was more than just everyone complaining about the early drill. Suddenly a voice came over the loud speaker.

"This is your Captain, Captain Gonzalez speaking. I have an important announcement to make so please be quiet and listen very carefully." "The ship has been commandeered. I and my crew are being held as hostages and there are several men aboard the ship, who have taken command of the ship. You will know them by the orange colored overalls they are wearing. They are armed. Do not attempt to resist what they tell you to do. They have promised not to harm anyone who obeys their instructions." "The meals will be served at the normal times. There will be several exceptions to how the trip is run. The casinos will be closed. There will be no room service. The movies and bingo and other entertainment will be canceled. You will be allowed on deck for two hours during the time that breakfast is served. After that you will return to your cabin. I understand that our destination has been changed.

" I have not been told where we are headed." "Another thing all, cell phones must be turned in to the stewards. I have been told that anyone caught with a cell phone will suffer severe consequences.

The warning of course went unheeded with a couple of passengers and they were caught red handed. They were hustled away and not seen again. It was assumed that they were isolated in a secured cabin. It was not long before Alex learned that there were some very wealthy people on board. As a matter of fact they were on the board of the New York Stock Exchange. Could this have been the reason that the ship was hijacked?

"Where are we headed?"

" Surely they will pick us up on the radar screen as having moved off our course."

"Someone has to find out about the hijack, and then the United States will send warships after us."

The ship was only a few hours from Cuba and it took a heading toward the Island. Jim Feron was on his way to the laboratory when his cell phone went off. It was William Colin. "I want you to call me as soon as you get to the laboratory on one of our secure phone lines. Jim could feel the urgency in his voice and he sped toward Central Islip passing cars like they were standing still.

CHAPTER XXX

"What do you mean the ship is missing?" said Jim.

"It is missing and we haven't got a clue as to what happened. There was some attempt by someone on board to use their cell phone and a garbled communication was picked up in Guantanamo but they could not decipher it. The only words they could understand were"

"Ship taken ....Captain is being.........Don't know where.......then the phone went dead." "That doesn't sound good." said Jim. "Where is the last position that we know the ship was at, Latitude, Longitude." "They had the ship about fifty miles off of Cuba and we have asked the Cuban Government to assist in locating the ship.""They have agreed but their patrol boats have not found any trace of the ship." "If the ship sank, surely they would have had time to send out a May Day. It would have to been an explosion and she would have had to go down instantly. There is no indication of an explosion or anything like it."

"That did not happen and yet a ship doesn't disappear without a trace."

Colin said "We are waiting on a reading from our satellites. They should pick up what happened to the ship."

"When will we have that information." said Jim.""The photos are being transmitted to our laboratories in Washington and I will have them within an hour. I'll let you know then." Jim tried to keep himself busy for the hour that would pass until Colin called him back .It proved to be more than an hour. The hour passed and then two hours and then three hours."What the hell is going on." he thought.

After four hours, the phone rang and it was William Colin.

"Jim, we think that the Cubans have the ship."

"The ship disappears off the coast of Cuba." "It is last seen at a port which is a port for oil tankers and other ships.

"The ships observed are several oilers, tankers and a dry dock berthed there."

"But there is still no sign of the Carioca II."

"More satellite pictures keep coming in and are being analyzed." "I'll keep you informed."

"Thank you, sir." said Jim.

Colin called again after another three hours. "We have a strange situation."

"The ship was only miles from a port in Cuba and it disappeared. We have counted the number of ships berthed and their are five large tankers and two carrier type barges"

"I am sending the satellite photos on to you. Maybe "Investicom" can do something for us. What do you think?"

Jim got the photos by courier and he studied them. "Wait a minute, look at this" he said as he showed them to his son, John.

"In this photo taken with the Carioca II fifty miles from the port you can count four tankers and two barges. Then the Carioca II disappears and now there are five tankers and two barges. Where did the fifth tanker come from?" Jim and his son, John discussed using the Photo Recognition program on the photos.

"This could be a real test of it's capability." said John. "We have to have a very recent shot from the satellite." Jim called Colin and it was arranged to project a live image to the laboratory of the port and the ships berthed there.

They had to wait until the satellite passed over the area and then they could view the image on a large projection screen set up in the lab. They were waiting when they received an unexpected guest. William Colin had flown to the laboratory. He wanted to see the results of the experiment.

The big screen was on and showing a lot of static transmissions when all of a sudden the view of the North American Continent came in to view. Now it was over the Caribbean. "Can we zoom in on the island of Cuba?" said Colin. The zoom feature closed in on Cuba, slowly picking up the area where the ships were in port.

There they were the four tankers and the two barges. Now the program focused in on the ships. It took about thirty minutes for "Investicom" to determine that one of the ships was a phony. "The ship berthed third from the left is not a tanker." said John.

"It is the Carioca II."

"It is camouflaged somehow."

"How could they do that?" said Colin. "They have something over it or they've changed it somehow so it looks like a tanker, but it is not. It's the Carioca II.

"Investicom" had done it's job and now it was up to Colin and his group to figure out what had to be done. "Those sons of bitches, they've got that ship and they're giving us a bunch of bullshit that they don't know where it is."" I'm flying back to Washington right now and I'll get back to you. He was cursing as he left the lab. "Son of a bitch, bastard, ..."

Jim and his son, John just looked at each other as he left. Jim looked at his son with a lot of respect. "My son." he said

"He figured it out." He was so proud. They closed up the lab and went home, but before the went home they stopped and had a couple of martinis at Tellers in Islip and then decided to stay and have a steak. They could only wait for Colin to call them for the next move in the operation.

The next day, they all went to work in the lab and they still hadn't heard any word about what was going to be done as far as the kidnapping of the Carioca II. They all worked on new programs and it seemed like they worked way over the usual eight or nine hours that they usually spent at the lab. The phone never rang and then around eight o'clock they all left and had a late dinner. Jim got home in time to watch the Monday Night Football game. He watched as his team the "Giants" were getting beaten by the "Bears" then all of a sudden they rallied and it looked like they might win the game. He got out a bottle of VO and poured himself a shot with a large glass of Ginger Ale on the side. "Come on lets go" he yelled. The Giants moved down the field and they were behind by four points with one minute and 20 seconds on the clock. They got to the twenty with 35 seconds on the clock. First down on the twenty. On the first play they lost two yards on a running play.

"Damn, throw the ball." said Jim.

Now there was twenty seconds to play and it was third down and seven. The quarterback faded back and was thrown for a loss. "Shit." said Jim. Fourth down and twenty seven with thirteen seconds left to play. It would be a pass.

"Of course throw the ball." The quarterback faded back, he dropped the ball and then picked it up and started to run. He ran around end. He made it to the ten and dodged away from tacklers, he moved inside and headed for the goal. He jumped over the last tackler and scored. Jim leaped to his feet knocking over his shot glass of VO and the Ginger Ale chaser. The Giants had won.

"Way to go." He murmured. He sat down and poured himself another drink and watched the post game show. He never made it through the wrap up. He fell asleep in the chair as they reviewed the winning play.

He slept deeply. His first dream was that he was the quarterback for the Giants and he was moving the team down the field. But it was like a lot of dreams. Whenever he got the ball, he couldn't seem to run. His feet wouldn't move and he wasn't able to throw the ball either. Then he woke up and went to the bathroom. He got undressed and went to bed properly.

It didn't take long for him to resume his sleep. This time he dreamed that he was on a cruise ship and walking on the deck. Alex was there and he beckoned to him to follow him to the bar. Jim tried to catch up to him but never managed to. Then Elizabeth appeared and she was sitting at a table by the bar. "Hy honey, I've been waiting for you." He couldn't seem to speak. "Honey, I want to tell you something Anne is alive and she is waiting for you." He turned away from her and then when he turned back , Elizabeth was gone. The rest of the dream was hazy and then he woke up. It was 6:00 A.M. His coffee machine was automatically making his coffee. He poured himself a cup and looked out of the window to see if his morning paper had been delivered. It had. He stepped outside and gathered up his paper and read it as he had his morning coffee.

The headline read, "Cruise Ship suspected kidnapped by Cubans."

"State Department demands answers from Fidel Castro."

He read on. Castro denies any involvement by the Cuban Government relative to the disappearance of the Carioca II. turned on Eye Witness News and they were interviewing relatives of the people on board the ship. They were demanding an answer about the disappearance. There were experts who commented that the ship could have exploded or sank without a trace. Then a representative of the Cuban Government came on and denied that his government was involved. Jim got on the phone with his old friend Hector Thomson.

"How are you, Hector. I have a very big favor to ask of you. You are going to think I am crazy but I want you to check into the accident involving Anne Fulton. I have a premonition that she was not the passenger in the taxi that had the accident."

" Jim, let it go, she's dead, they identified her property."

"Please, Hector , I can't tell you what is motivating me, Please check further." "I wouldn't do this for anyone except you." "I will have to pull some strings, because the case is closed and well I'll get back to you. Meanwhile what are you doing?" "Can't tell you Hector." "Oh, sorry, I should have known."

"I'll get back to you, stay well old friend."

Jim was happy. His old friend would check and maybe the dreams would go away. Meanwhile, he was concerned about Alex and the ship. What the hell was going on? He was to find out soon.

CHAPTER XXXI

Jim got a phone call from Colin. He wanted him in Washington. There was to be a conference regarding the missing ship. Jim wondered if Tom Bragg would be there. He found out soon enough that he would.

The conference room was filled with military and intelligence personnel. Colin chaired the meeting.

"Ladies and Gentlemen, I don't have to tell you that nothing you learn inside of this room is to be remotely discussed outside. This meeting is Top Secret and you will learn that the information you are about to receive is only disseminated to a select few. If you consider that a compliment you are right it is."

"You will notice that there is a folder in front of you. This folder contains information which will help you to understand this briefing. There will be no note taking. Any information you need to remember will be in these packets and they are not to leave this room"

Colin looked directly into the eyes of each and every one sitting at the table. He spoke slowly and softly. "The Cubans have the Carioca II." "We know that from the marvelous work of our computer and satellite operation." "We have confronted them with what we know.""A strange thing happened when our Department of State had a meeting with their people." "They admitted they have the ship. It is unharmed and the passengers are all well and in good shape, according to them." "They originally wanted to hold the ship as hostage as a trade off for lifting the embargo."

"This has changed. Their whole position has softened."

"They are willing to release the ship but first they want a meeting between our Intelligence people and their DGI (General Intelligence Directorate of the Ministry of the Interior and the Military Counterintelligence Department of the Ministry of the Revolutionary Armed Forces. "We will assemble a small group of Intelligence operatives and also I want Mr. Feron and Tom Bragg to attend this conference in Cuba."

"It was at this time that Jim saw Tom who was sitting at the other end of the table. Tom gave him a wink as Colin mentioned the names of who would attend the conference.

"Although we were able, so we thought, to force their hand about the Carioca II, it seems that they were about to disclose that they had the ship anyway. They do not want it leaked to the press that they hi-jacked the ship. It is to be disclosed through our Press Relations people that the ship had a steering problem and put in to a Cuban port and of course before they could disclose this they had to be sure it was not some sort of a covert spy operation and that the ship was truly disabled."

"I think we may be able to get away with this story. The passengers believe that they were hi-jacked, however they will be told that the ship had to be taken for security reasons."

"They have emphasized that this meeting be held, although they are still willing to surrender the ship. Because of their willingness to cooperate, we have to believe that they have something very important to put on the table." "We'll see."

Plans were formulated for the group to fly into Guantanamo and from there they would meet with the Cuban DGI.

Jim and Tom had a chance to chat on the flight about their respective families. Jim asked about Linda. "She's fine, very happy." said Tom. "Good, I'm glad."They landed at Guantanamo and were billeted with the Marine Officers.

Jim and Tom had a chance to have a drink at the Officer's Club and discuss their former adventures.

"I wonder what they have up their sleeve." said Tom. "They seem like they want to be sincere but based on their past I still don't trust them." William Colin was to chair the conference and his presence indicated that it was regarded as very significant.

The meeting with the DGI was set up for the next day and it was conducted at Guantanamo. The Cuban officials passed through the gate at 8:00 A.M. They drove through in a black Mercedes. There were five of them.

The conference started off slowly with a lot of pleasantries passed between both parties. Coffee and rolls and donuts were on the table and the Cubans seemed to relish the continental breakfast that was put out. They especially enjoyed the jelly donuts, spilling powdered sugar on to their clothes.

After all of this the conference got on in earnest. Colin spoke "You took our ship and now you are willing to give it back.""What do you want in return?" " The one Cuban who was wearing a military uniform spoke. He spoke in fluent English. " My name is General Alejandro Martinez and I will be the spokesperson for the Cuban delegation to this conference

" First, We did take your ship and for that we apologize."

"We have a desperate economic situation in Cuba and we need American products such as corn, grain, rice, farm products and we want the Embargo to be lifted and we want to resume normal relations with the United States. The ship will be returned as soon as possible."

"There are no conditions on it's return. We have something t hat you will find very interesting and highly important to relate to you."

"You can believe that the information that we have is true and was obtained through our Intelligence sources."

"What if I say, we just want our ship back and let it go at that."

"That would be an extremely foolish move on your part."

"All we ask is that you listen to what we have and then make up your own minds if it is valuable enough for your government to consider removing the Embargo and having full scale trade and diplomatic relations with our country."

"Can we be fairer than that?"

Colin looked at General Martinez, but this time his expression was that of "maybe this man is telling the truth." "General Martinez, why don't we adjourn the meeting for today. I would like to talk to some people and then let's meet tomorrow, okay?" That's fine and by the way would you mind bringing those donuts again? My personnel really seemed to enjoy them." "We will have them and some others that I'm sure you will enjoy. We'll see you tomorrow. Have a nice day, sir." General Martinez rose from the table and gave a slight bow to Colin and his delegation left.

Jim looked over at Tom Bragg and they met at the door.

"Let's go for a Martini." said Jim.

"I'm with you." and Tom and Jim sat down at the bar in the Officer's club and discussed the meeting. They wondered what the Cubans had that they wanted to trade. "I hate to say this, but I kind of like this General Martinez, he seems sincere." said Jim.

"Me too."

The meeting was held the next day and this time they had jelly donuts, glazed donuts and some Lindser Tarts, which went very quickly. "What do you call these?" said Martinez. "They are called "Lindser Tarts." "You must give our people the recipe."

Colin led off the meeting with a short speech. "I have been in touch with some high level officials in Washington and we appreciate your willingness to return the ship."

"We would like that process to begin today." "Second, our intelligence officials will sit down with your people relative to the information that you say that you have."

"Arrangements should be made this morning to start this dialogue immediately." "As far as the lifting of the Embargo, we make no promises but our State Department has agreed to have a conference starting the beginning of next month in Washington. Your people are invited to come and a serious discussion will take place as to the resumption of normal relations with your country." General Martinez smiled and nodded. He was obviously very happy with the possibility of normal relations.

The meeting was short and arrangements were made for the Intelligence people to get together. Colin took Jim and Tom aside as the meeting broke up and asked them to stay so he could speak with both of them. "I want both of you to be part of this Intelligence conference. I have a premonition that it may require your expertise and also our old friend "Investicom." Jim and Tom were directed to the Intelligence operatives and told that they would be notified of the first meeting. They went back to the Officer's club and had their usual evening libation.

They were contacted at the bar by the Intelligence people. The meeting was set for tomorrow. They had only two drinks, had a steak and went to their rooms early. They both wanted to be on their toes for the meeting. No fuzzy heads for this meeting.

The meeting was early and the Cubans wasted no time in disseminating the information that they had uncovered. The Intelligence Officer started with a caveat

"The source of this information can not be divulged by either sides."" It is simply this."

"Al Quaida has developed a plan to kill the President of the United States, The British Prime Minister and the Holy Father." "We obtained this information through sources that we developed during our operation in Angola.""The plan is very sophisticated and we have an inside source." "The plan is to kill all three of them at the same time and the same date." "They have picked a significant date and the time will be the same in the United States, Britain and Rome." "Our intelligence sources have done a fantastic job."

"Preventing this horrific act will have to be coordinated by your people."

"So far, we know that the killings are set for next month, so we have little time to prepare."

"Please read the information in the folders, we have prepared and we will meet again, tomorrow, early."

"Thank you." The Cubans got up and left the room. Another meeting was set for early the next day.

As they were leaving the room, General Martinez came over to Jim and Tom.

"Mr. Feron, Would you come with me?"He led them to another room, which was guarded by a Marine Corporal. They entered and a man got up from an easy chair. It was Alex. They rushed together and Jim hugged him. "How are you?"

"I'm okay"

"I said a few prayers to our old friend St. Anthony and of course he came through again. "Thank you General." The General nodded and left. Tom said "Let's go have a drink." "I thought you would never ask." said Alex and the three of them walked out arm in arm and straight to the Officer's Club.

CHAPTER XXXII

There were more meetings and the plan was disclosed by the Cubans. It was apparent that their source was still active and gaining more intelligence every day.

Thus far, his or her information provided was that there would be three assassination attempts. One on the President of the United States, the second on the Prime Minister of Great Britain and the third on the Pope.

The attempts would be made simultaneously and it appeared that they had the means to break through the private security in order to accomplish their missions. The date of the attempt was still in doubt. It would be a significant date. An anniversary or a religious holiday either Islamic or Christian. This had them all looking at the calendars for possibilities.

Jim returned to Long Island with Alex and Tom came with the to attempt some theories with "Investicom" First they tried putting in all dates into the computer which could be possibilities . The holidays, religious days, birthdays, anniversaries both historic and tragic. They came up with a multitude of possibilities. They put them on a chart up on the wall. It was a large series of calendars ranging for the next three months with the holiday or anniversary in the square denoting the day of the month. Then they gathered information which showed the itineraries of the three men on each day at each hour for the next three months. Where they would be, all three of them at the same time each day. This went on another chart, much bigger than the other one.

"This place is starting to look like NASA." said Tom Bragg as he came in one morning. They worked long hours from early morning to late at night. The pressure was on. They had to find out what the plan was and when it would be put into operation. It would have been easy to just put all three of them in isolation, but that was unthinkable. It would close down two governments and the Catholic Church. They were alerted by their respective Intelligence Sections of the danger but alerts could not be given to their security personnel, in the event that one of them was involved in the attempt. "They must not know that we know what they are up to." said William Colin.

Jim decided to take the Personnel Files of all of the Security Personnel for the three men and incorporate them in a composite file through

"Investicom" This was a huge job. There were hundreds of people who were involved in the day to day security for the President, Prime Minister and the Pope. All of the information was gathered through the State Department and Colin.

The files arrived by plane and in file boxes stacked several feet high. Alex, Tom, and Jim went to work with Jim's kids incorporating the files into the data base. They were given five secretaries from the Pentagon, who worked through the day entering data, After five days, all of the information had been entered and now the computer could go to work. It would sort, compare and profile all of the personnel. The results of this would take another two days. Once the clerical end of the operation was completed all they could now was wait. The secretaries were sent back to Washington, but not before Alex, Tom and Jim threw them a little party. They had a buffet and some beer and wine. Everyone had a good time. Jim and Tom were talking standing near the buffet with their plastic plates full of baked ziti, sausage and peppers, baked clams and Italian Bread. They juggled all of this with a plastic cup of wine from the different bottles that they got for the party. "Look over there." said Tom. Jim looked and saw Alex in deep conversation with a very attractive secretary. "He looks like he's taken with her." "Hey, he's human, she's very nice looking." "How old do you think she is, Tom" "I'd say about fifty." Tom and Jim chuckled at the thought of a budding romance between Alex and one of the secretaries. They were not far from being wrong because Alex asked the woman for her phone number in Virginia and she gave it to him. She had told him that she was a widow and worked now for the government. Jim asked Alex

"Hey what were you doing with that young gal at the party ?

"She's not that young and she's very nice and nice looking too, don't you think? Jim

"Am I too old to meet someone."

"Nah, I'm just breaking them, Alex. Go for it. She looked like a nice lady."

"Are you going to see her again?"

"Yes, as a matter of fact I am going to Virginia this weekend to have dinner with her." True to his word, Alex did go to Virginia and have dinner with the lady, who was named Virginia. They made fun of it. "Virginia from Virginia."

The next day she took him around Washington and showed him some of the sights. He had never seen the Marine Corps Monument all lit up at night. "That is a beautiful dedication to some very brave men." he said. "My dad died at Iwo Jima, and this monument is very special to me." Alex saw Virginia to her door and she kissed him goodnight. "I really like you, Alex." she said. "I love you." said Alex. She stepped back and then kissed him again. "I'll call you tomorrow." "I have to work tomorrow." Take the day off." he said.

"Okay, I will." and they parted.

Alex returned to his hotel room and there was a message waiting for him. "Return to the laboratory tomorrow. Very important. Jim." He knew what that meant. "Investicom" had done it again and he was needed to view the results. He got a flight out at two in the morning. He was fortunate enough to get a shuttle flight. He was back in Long Island and shaved and showered by 5 AM.

"Here's our lover boy." said Tom as he walked in the door.

"You're just in time to review the results of our latest search." The search had produced reams of paper from the printer, but certain pages were highlighted and the results were startling. Out of all of the personnel involved in protecting the respective individuals being the President, the Prime Minister of Britain and the Pope. They came up with three individuals who had twin brothers. Then looking into the backgrounds of the twins, "Investicom" found that they all had disappeared. The twin who had a brother who was a Secret Service Agent went Missing In Action in Vietnam and was never found. The twin who was a bodyguard for the Prime Minister of Britain was part of the inspection team for the U.N. That made inspections in Iraq.

He repeatedly had reported that the sites were clean and appeared on CNN as very sympathetic to the regime. He left the Inspection team and was living in Saudi Arabia according to last reports.

The second twin who was the brother of a Swiss Guard, assigned to guard the Pope, was married to a Korean woman and had made several trips to Korea with her to "visit" her family.

They all sat down with Colin and went over the results of "Investicom"'s search."What's your theory?" said Colin. Tom said he thought it looked like a strong lead into what they might be planning and how they might go about it. Jim said

"They could use the twins as substitute body guards."

"What and where are these people right now?"

"Does anybody know.?"

"I've got some people working on it as we speak." said Colin.

Jim went back to the laboratory and sat down with his kids and Alex and they discussed the latest developments. Jim's daughter Elizabeth was sitting with them and offhandedly said "Why don't you use the "Facial Recognition Program"

"You could compare the people who have been assigned to the bodyguard details of the President, Prime Minister and Pope with the current bodyguards and make sure that the twins have not taken over the positions

"That's a great idea, Elizabeth." "Boy am I glad I had you assigned to "Investicom" said Jim. He got on the telephone and called Colin and the comparison would be put into effect immediately. After all they did not know how much time they had before the assassinations would take place.

CHAPTER XXXIII

The call came in from Colin. He was very excited. "Fly to Washington today. We have more information from the Cubans as to when the assassinations are to take place." Jim, Alex and Tom got down to Washington as fast as they could. They went into the conference room where everyone was already seated and waiting. "Gentlemen, our new found friends have come up with the information that we need. Their source tells them that the date and time of the assassinations has to do with the "Sacred Months" of the Quran." "I will yield the floor to General Martinez." General Martinez looked around the room and then he spoke. "Our operative has obtained information that indicates that the assassination attempts will take place after the "Sacred Months" taken from the verses in Quran." " The Quran, for those of you not familiar says that ring the "Sacred Months" aggression may be met by an equivalent response. If they attack you, you may retaliate by inflicting equitable retribution. You shall observe God and know that God is with the righteous. Once the Sacred Months are past and they refuse to make peace, you may kill the idol worshipers when you encounter them, punish them and resist every move they make." " The four Sacred Months are Zul-Hijjah, Muharram, Safar and Rabi I.

(They designate the 12th, 1st, 2nd and 3rd months." "They have interpreted that once the four months are over, which according to what we know, will be in April, sometime then, the assassinations will take place. Today's date is March15th.""How prophetic, The ides of March."

"Gentlemen, we will continue to inform you of any new developments as our operative obtains them. Thank you and Good Day."

"April, Jesus, that's only two weeks away." said Jim. Colin waited until the Cuban delegation had left and then he spoke. "I have some bad news. The personnel records that we needed to compare regarding the twins have been destroyed in a fire." "We are looking into the possibility of it being suspicious."

" Anyway, we can't use your program to compare photos of the bodyguards in the Secret Service against the possible switch to the twin brother." "And now I've heard that in the UK their records have had a mishap also." "I'm afraid to check on the Vatican."

"Can we get any home movies of the Secret Service bodyguards or even newsreel photos?" "We probably can, but it will take time and we don't have a lot of time."

"I'll put some people on it and get back to you."said Colin. He looked a little grim as he spoke. The pressure was on.

All that Jim, Tom and Alex could do was wait for more data.

"What else can we do to identify the assassins?" said Alex.

"We could be barking up the wrong tree." said Jim. Tom said "I have a hunch that you guys have hit on the right solution."

"What else have we got?"

"Let's go have dinner and a drink." said Tom "I'll even buy."

"That's all I had to hear." said Jim.

They left and had a nice dinner at the Jon Thomas Inne in West Islip. After that they had a couple of after dinner drinks and then went home. No one did much talking. There was a somber mood about the evening. Jim was very depressed and his kids who went to dinner with them noticed.

"Dad, don't take it so hard. You're doing the best you can."

"Yeah and with your help." he said. "Dad, we'll get 'em, don't worry." He smiled at the two of them, kissed them, and said Good Night.

He slept deeply and again had a dream about his wife and the kids when they were just little. Elizabeth was as beautiful as when he first met her. She was sitting in the laboratory with him and working with him on the computer. She looked up and said "Honey, the answer to your problem will come from a home video taken when the Pope came into New York and said mass at Yankee Stadium. The President was there and so was the Prime Minister. Look to the left of the Pope. There is a man sitting in civilian clothes. The video pans to the President and his bodyguards and next to him the Prime Minister. He woke up in a sweat and immediately called Washington. He got one of Colin's aides and asked him if any home videos had been recovered, especially those of the Pope's visit to New York. No none had been.

"It was just a dream." he thought, a tease."

"No credibility to it." He went back to sleep.

The next day they got a call from Colin. All of the security personnel for the President, Prime Minister and the Pope had been changed. There were all new bodyguards. Would that end the assassination attempt? Did they have an alternative plan? Now they would have to figure out what that plan could be. Never the less, they proceeded with the "twin" theory and obtained videos of the former bodyguards to compare with the most recent photos. It was determined that a switch had been made. The bodyguards were the "twins". They were all the missing "twins" . Very quietly all of these people were taken into custody. They were subjected to intense interrogation but not one of them would crack. Finally one of them broke his silence and he related the story of the transfer. All of the twins had ties to Communist countries that had been in conflict with the United States at one time. The twin who was a bodyguard for the President and had a brother who was missing in Vietnam was switched after contact was made with the Secret Service man from a member of the Missing in Action Group, who allegedly were campaigning for the return of missing service men in Vietnam. They told him that they had information about his brother. He believed them and went to a meeting in Los Angeles. He was told not to inform anyone, because it would jeopardize negotiations underway to return his brother. It was in LA that he was kidnaped and the switch made. The Prime Minister's bodyguard was switched on a trip to Saudi Arabia made by the Prime Minister of Britain. He was taken prisoner at a banquet. He told one of his colleagues that he was going to the bathroom and it was there that they kidnapped him and made the switch.

The Pope's Swiss bodyguard was kidnapped in Korea on a trip with his Korean wife. They were both taken at a hotel that they were staying, while visiting her relatives in Seoul. The whereabouts of the prisoners was not known. The informant believed that they were all killed. Once all of the men assigned to the President, Prime Minister and the Pope had been changed, the group planning the assassination knew because they could not longer be in touch with their people. The cat was out of the bag. The question was how would they proceed with their plan. More important was to find out the exact of the attempts.

"Investicom" was put to the test. It was one of the first times that it had failed to come up with the information that they had wanted.

"It's because we are not inserting the proper data for it to evaluate." said Jim. "We've got to get something that it can use to determine the date we want to look at. This was the biggest puzzle for all of them. Without the proper data they were at a loss. Jim was staring up at the big chart that they had prepared as a result of "Investicom's"research into important dates. The one date that stood out was May 14. This was the birthday of Mohammed. More important it was only days away. "Maybe we are putting too much into the synchronization of dates." He thought. "They are making it very simple. They will strike on Mohammed's birthday." He made a call to Colin in Washington and conveyed his thoughts. Colin said

"We have thought about that date too and we are going to take precautions for the activities of the President,Prime Minister and the Pope for that date."

"But thanks Jim for calling. I always have time for you and your colleagues."

CHAPTER XXXIV

It came down to relying on the Cubans again. They got a message from their informant that related to the date of the assassination. It was cryptic but it referred to "his" birthday. That day would be the 14th of May. When Colin found out he called Jim and told him. "We may have guessed right. They are talking about "his" birthday as the day when "we will strike" using their words. Now all preparations must be made to safeguard the three men, who no matter where they were or what they were doing would be "targets".

The President had scheduled a meeting with some Boy Scouts in the morning in the Oval Room. In the afternoon, he was supposed to attend a luncheon being held by the International Red Cross in the D.C. Convention Center. The Security for this event was heavy. The luncheon was scheduled for 1:00 P.M. It would be 6:00 P.M. In London.

The Prime Minister was leaving Parliament about this time and he would have dinner with the Ambassador to St. James Court. They would dine at the plush Le Meridien Grosvenor Hotel in Park Lane. It was to be a private dinner with members of their respective staffs.

At 7:00 P.M. Rome time, the Pope was scheduled to appear on the balcony overlooking St. Peter's square and give audience to thousands of people. And so the scene was set for the biggest assassination attempt in history. Jim waited with Alex and Tom and Jim's kids at the laboratory.

They were all sitting on the edge of their seats. It seemed like whenever the phone rang they all jumped. They all wanted so much to be a part of the preparations to prevent a monumental tragedy. They wanted instructions but none came. So they sat and paced and worked harmless programs in the computer, just keeping "Investicom" ready like a "pinch hitter" waiting in the on deck circle.

When the phone rang everyone jumped as if they were stung by bees. It was Colin and he had information for them. They were on a secure telephone line and Jim put on the speaker phone so they could all hear what he had to say.

"We've received information. This time it's from our own people. We have prisoners in Guantanamo and recently they received an opportunity to be visited by the Red Cross. One of the Red Cross workers was overheard speaking to one of the prisoners and he passed along information to him that "we are going to celebrate the prophet's birthday."

"Keep up your spirits and your resolve. You will see how we celebrate the birth of the prophet." We have pictures of this worker and we got some DNA from a cigarette butt he used. We could have arrested him, but it was felt that he might lead us to more of them. We want you to put the info into "Investicom"

"You will receive the packet within the hour. I don't have to tell you that we have to work as quickly as possible. Good Luck." No sooner than he hung up than the plane arrived and the packet was delivered. The information was quickly fed into the computer.

"Investicom" produced some amazing results. The Red Cross man's true identity was revealed. He had worked as an embassy employee for the Indian Government. He had assignments in Rome and London also. He was further identified as Al Quaida. He was being surveilled from the time he left Guantanamo and he was followed to Washington D.C. The surveillance was lost in the vicinity of The Grand Hyatt Hotel, which was just steps away from the Convention Center. Secret Service men and other White House Security Agents were all over the area seeking their lost prey. Unnoticed, he joined the delegation of the International Red Cross entering the Convention Center. He was picked up on one of the overhead surveillance cameras in the banquet room. Now he was under constant surveillance from cameras. One of the Secret Service Supervisors advised

"Pick him up." "Do it quickly and without any disturbance to the room." Before they could move to "pick him up", the President entered the room and everyone rose to applaud. They couldn't get through the crowd to get to their man. What kind of a weapon or device could he have? All of the persons entering the room had to go through strict security before sitting down at the tables. His table was situated to the left of the dais and close to where the President would be. The only weapons available were the cutlery on the tables. What was the plan? They were all seated when the President entered the room. They all took their seats as the President approached the podium. Two of the Secret Servicemen had managed to station themselves between the man's table and the dais. He saw what was happening and he got up and then like a half back he twisted and dodged to get around the Secret Service. He had a handkerchief in his hand. The Secret Service took him down and he dropped the handkerchief, which had some white powder in it. It splashed on the floor of the room. One of the Secret Service men ran into the kitchen off of the banquet room and got a plastic cake cover. He ran back and put it over the white powder. Meanwhile, the President was ushered out of the room, into a waiting limousine and driven away from the center. The police evacuated the room as quickly as they could and the room was sealed off. They had some environmental specialists take over the room and they recovered the powder for testing.

The powder turned out to be Anthrax.

At the same time only London time, the Prime Minister was sitting down at his table with the Ambassador to St. James. "Investicom" was being utilized to scan the room. One of it's functions was an optical scanner recently developed in New Mexico that would analyze gases. It had a scanner that could analyze through a Polychromator chip a lethal gas. This chip could mimic the infrared spectrum of any gas. When the chip would hit an identical spectrum, it could identify the gas. In a particular instance it could identify a poison gas in the area. This is what it did. As the VIPs were seated and awaiting their usual "rubber chicken" dinner, the poison gas was being sent into the room via the heating, air conditioning ventilating systems. "Investicom" detected it almost immediately and the Prime Ministers's Security forces were alerted and they broke out gas masks for the Prime Minister and his guests , themselves and all of the people in the room were ushered out and then the room sealed off. Two of the three attempts had been thwarted.

It was 7:00 P.M. In Rome when the third attempt was about to take place. The Pope came out onto the balcony for his weekly audience in front of an assemblage of tourists and worshipers. They all waited very patiently until the French doors on the opened and the Pope emerged from inside the balcony. His hands were extended as was his usual greeting stance to the crowd. The people in the square started to clap and they chanted "Papa". The Pope stood motionless with his hands raised at his sides. Meanwhile "Investicom" was at work scanning the crowd with a new program designed to find anyone through an infra red sensor that was carrying and kind of a firearm. The computer scanned slowly through the crowd but there were thousands of people in the square and it was taking a lot of time to go to check. It was though there was a giant metal detector such as the ones placed in airports, courts and buildings. Only this was scanning a large body of individuals. It was picking up all sorts of objects that could be determined as pistols ,but that was not what they were really looking for. A pistol used at that distance was not what the terrorists would use.

They needed something much bigger.

Then the computer zeroed in on an individual, however this person had already begun to make his move. The man dropped to his knees and from a suitcase he took out a rifle which was broken down in to three parts. He immediately started to assemble the rifle. It was strange because no one was paying any attention to what he was doing. They were all focused on the Pope. "Investicom" had alerted Security forces in the area, however, the man was in the middle of a large assembly and it would take time to get to him. Too much time. And then he got up and stood on the suitcase to elevate himself. He had the rifle assembled and he was aiming at the balcony. He had a telescopic sight and as he looked down the sight, the cross hairs had the Pope's chest in the middle. He fired and then he fired again. The bullets struck the Pope in the chest and he went down. The crowd was in a panic from the shots and the man had little trouble getting through the crowd especially since he was holding a rifle which was thrust out from his waist. No one wanted to challenge this crazy man with the rifle.

Father John Connally was the closest person to the man with the rifle and he was the only one who approached him. The man broke into a run, knocking people down as he ran through the square. Father John had been a Halfback with the Notre Dame Football team before he went to the Seminary and studied for the priesthood. He was after the man running as best he could with his priest's garb. He stopped for a minute to remove his smock. Under it he had on a sweatshirt and sweat pants. The only thing that was a benefit was that he had worn sneakers that day.

"No one will notice me wearing these under the smock." he thought.

"And I'll be more comfortable standing as long as we will have to waiting for the Pope to come out onto the balcony."

Now the man was out in the open and sprinting away from the square. Now the chase took place on the Via Dei Corridori, which led from St.Peter's square. The man still had the rifle slung around his neck. Behind him was Father John, breathing very hard and not gaining any ground. Then the man made a huge mistake. He knelt and turned to fire at the priest, who was not gaining any ground. The man thought him to be a threat and wanted to take him out, so he cocked the rifle and aimed at the oncoming runner. Father John saw the man in position to fire at him and so he started to zig zag like a broken field runner. The first shot whistled past his ear, then a second shot went through his legs. Frustrated that he had not hit his prey, the man got up and started to run again. But now he had lost ground on the priest. Being much younger and much leaner, he made up some of the ground he had lost. Father John was starting to poop out and he knew it. He huffed and puffed and then he started to pray.

"Please, Dear Jesus, help me to capture this satanic person, who would harm our holy father."

Then it happened, he got a second wind and now he was gaining. He was twenty yards away, then ten, then five. The man was starting to feel the strain of the chase and he was slowing down. With one huge leap, Father John tackled the man and brought him down. Both of them crashed to the pavement. The rifle went flying off, yards away. The man could not put up a battle, because the tackle and the impact of the two bodies hitting the ground had taken it's toll on his body. Father John, however, was really pumped up and he raised the man from the ground and pushed him up against a nearby building. He held him there until some Italian Carabiniere arrived to take the man into custody.

They took the man into custody and asked Father John to accompany them to the Italian Police Station.

They were all met there with some of Colin's people, plus investigators from the Carabiniere and the Swiss Guard. The assailant was taken into a interrogation room. Father John gave a statement and was checked out by a physician and then he was free to go. He was distraught however, because he had seen the Pope struck by two bullets. Before he left, one of the investigators from the Carabiniere spoke with him. "Father, do not fear, Il Papa is fine." "Believe me, he is not hurt."

"How?"

" I saw the bullets hit him in the chest." "Have you ever heard of Madame Tussaud's Wax Museum?"

"I've heard of it." "As a matter of fact I've been there." said Father

"Well the figure you saw on the balcony was a robot of the Pope. We had it programmed to walk out on the balcony." " We had information that there would be an attempt on the Pope's life, so we took the precaution of having the robot appear on the balcony. From that distance, no one could determine that it was not actually thePope." Father John just looked dumbfounded at the police officer.

Then he left. They had retrieved his smock from the square and so he was back "in uniform". The police had not been inactive. A search of the entire area uncovered a van parked by the Museum Di Castel Sant Angelo. There were three men inside and they were fully armed. The Carabiniere surrounded the vehicle and arrested the three without a fight.

Back in Long Island at the laboratory, Jim and his colleagues waited for information regarding all three of the attempts. It was not long before an excited and happy William Colin called and relayed all of the events which successfully saved the lives of three of the most important men in the world. Out came the champagne again and they all celebrated and hugged and danced and put on some music to mark the occasion.

CHAPTER XXXV

"Investicom" had come through again. It had helped save the lives of the President and the Prime Minister. It tried it's best in the case of the Pope, however other members of the team had come through to help save Il Papa.

Now it was time to evaluate the value of the computer. A survey was asked for and started by the team at the laboratory. Colin wanted the survey in order to gain more funds from the government for more research and development of "Investicom". Alex, Jim and his children all worked very hard on the survey. It was very important that the Congress be aware of the value and importance of the computer and vote money for more programs.

The report would take several weeks and then after it was submitted, a vacation for all. Alex went to Virginia to see Virginia.

"No more cruises for me for a while" he said.

The kids, John and Elizabeth went out west to Colorado. They wanted to enjoy some winter sports. Jim decided that he would go back to Great Britain. He would see his old friend, Hector.

Jim's plane landed on time and Hector was at the airport to meet him.

"How are you, been pretty busy, I hear."

"You and that computer of yours. I was part of the Prime Minister's entourage and they briefed me on the assassination attempt."

"I'm glad that we were able to prevent something Major." said Jim.

Hector drove him to a four star hotel in London and they dropped off his suitcases and immediately retreated to the hotel lounge. Hector seemed mysterious and Jim noticed it almost immediately.

"Hector, what's wrong. I sense something with you. What do you want to tell me?"

Hector took a long sip of his brandy and looked Jim right in the eye."Jim, you know the old saying I have good news and I have bad news?"

"Yeah. Go on."

"Well, the good news is that the credit card we found with blood on it at the scene of Anne's accident. It was not Anne's. This could have meant that the woman killed in the crash was not Anne. So we went further and we found that when she had her purse stolen some of the articles were never recovered and possibly one of her credit cards which had fallen into the wrong hands was in the possession of someone who was in the taxi when the crash occurred.""That's the good news, that she may be still alive."

"But the bad news is we have no idea where she might be."

"She's alive, I knew it, I can't tell you how I knew it because you'll think I'm nuts." "What do we have to go on to find her?" "Nothing." said Hector. "She left the hospital in a manner we don't know."

" We assumed that she left in a taxi and then the accident with her identification, I mean her credit card which identified her."

"And now the blood on the card isn't hers." " She has had episodes of amnesia and she could have had one when she wandered off.""Now she is someplace, in the United Kingdom and has a new identity."

After they had a few drinks, Jim and Hector parted and Jim went up to his room. He was troubled over the new developments. Hector promised to call him if there were any developments at all.

CHAPTER XXXVI

Anne Fulton was left alone in the hallway of the Nursing Home. She was sitting in a wheel chair, while the nurse went to see about her scheduled checkup for that day. She looked up and saw no one around. She stood up and walked toward the lobby. She had pajamas on and a robe over top. She looked down the hall and saw a laundry basket. It had some clothes piled in it. She got up and walked over to it. There was a dress folded in the basket. She took the dress, went into a broom closet and put on the dress. Then she walked out the door of the home. The receptionist was on the telephone and looked at her as she left. She called to her.

"Miss, do you have a pass?"

"If you do, please come back and leave it at the desk." Anne ignored her and just walked out the door. The receptionist just shook her head and continued with the phone call.

There were taxis and cars outside and a bus. She walked toward them.

A middle aged lady who was visiting saw her and said.

"The taxis are all taken dear, come on with me and let's get on this bus."

Anne got on the bus with the friendly old woman.

"Where are you going?"said the woman. "I have to meet a friend of mine in St. Andrews. We are spending a holiday there and playing golf." "Where is your luggage?" said the woman.

"Oh, she has everything.

""Were you visiting someone in the home"

"Yes, I have a friend who is there." The woman was a little curious about Anne's attitude but nevertheless when, she had now moved to the window seat. It was not tillseveral m iles down the road that Anne noticed the purse on the floor under the seat in front of her. The old woman had left her purse behind. Anne picked it up and started for the bus driver to let him know. "Excuse me sir, the woman on the bus left this purse behind." At that moment the bus had stopped and more passengers were coming on and asking for change. The bus driver didn't hear her. All he said was

"Lady, you're not supposed to talk to the driver, if you want to get off go to the rear of the bus."

Anne got pushed by the ongoing passengers and she found herself in front of the rear exit. She got off still holding the purse. When she got off, she noticed a taxi stand. She went to the nearest taxi and asked to be taken to the railroad station. The taxi driver said

"That'll be two pounds M'am." She realized that she had no money.

"Two pounds ma'am" he said again. She opened the purse and took out a five pound note and gave it to him. He gave her her change and they drove to the railroad station at Kings Cross. She purchased a ticket to Leuchars in Scotland. It was about 3:30 P.M. The train would arrive in Leuchars about 10 P.M. She dozed off while the train headed north to Scotland. A little while after the train got underway as soon as the a stewardess came around serving tea and small sandwiches. She took a cup of tea and a couple of cucumber sandwiches. She was famished. Then she resumed her nap.

The train pulled in about 10:30 P.M. And she got off looking around rather confusedly, when a taxi driver approached her and asked

"Need a ride, Miss?"

"Yes, I do."

"Is there a reasonable hotel nearby where I can spend the night. I"ll be going into St. Andrews in the morning

"I know a bed and breakfast, that I can take you to."

"Nice place, clean and they'll put you in a nice room and give you a hearty breakfast tomorrow."

"How does that sound to you?"

"Fine." said Anne.

"No luggage, miss?"

"No, a friend has all my things in St. Andrews. "

"I'd rather not disturb her tonight, so please take me to the place you described."

The taxi driver took her to the Bed and Breakfast and she checked in making the same excuses about luggage and telling the proprietors the same story about her friend in St. Andrews. She paid them in advance in cash, which she took from the purse again. After going to her room, it was almost no time before she went to sleep exhausted from the days events. A lot of things were going through her head. She was confused and scared but dared not tell anyone. The amnesia was controlling her in a strange way, but she didn't know it.

The next day she got up and went down to the breakfast room which was set up in the home. The woman owner, who was a middle aged Scotswoman named McBrerity asked her what kind of juice she wanted and did she want tea or coffee. Anne selected a glass of orange juice and a cup of tea.

"You just fix your tea and help yourself to some scones and marmalade, deary and I'll be in with your breakfast in just a moment. How do you like your eggs?"

"Scrambled, please."

Anne had just finished a scone with orange marmalade when Mrs. Mcbrerity came in with a large plate of scrambled eggs, sausages, a stewed tomato and some home fried potatoes. Anne ate her breakfast, had a second cup of tea and then got up to leave.

"Thank you, that was a wonderful breakfast.""See you again sometime."

"Is your friend expecting you?" said Mrs. McBrerity.

"Well, I wasn't expected today, I hope to kind of surprise her. Mrs. McBrerity had called a taxi for her, although it was only a short distance from the B&B to St. Andrews.

"Have a nice stay and come back again."

"I will."said Anne and went out to the taxi. It was only a five minute ride to St. Andrews and Anne got out on the main street which led to the golf course.

Now a surge of confusion overtook her.

"What am I doing here?"

"Oh yes, I am supposed to meet Elaine and have a golf holiday." She was going back in time in her mind. But then she couldn't remember where Elaine would meet her so she got upset and went into a small coffee shop and sat down. The waitress came over and asked her for her order. Anne just stared into space.

"Are you alright honey?" said the waitress. She could see that Anne was troubled and she appeared to be ill. "I'll bring you a cup of coffee, okay?" The waitress kept looking over at Anne as she served the other patrons of the café. Then she decided to go over.

"Listen, I hope you don't think I'm nosey or pushy, but I get off in a couple of minutes, why don't you come with me and maybe I can help you in some way. Okay?"

Anne nodded her head and sipped her coffee.

The waitress, Terry Murphy, finished her shift and took Anne with her to her apartment which was off the main drag in St. Andrews. She sat her down and started to ask her about herself. She could tell that Anne was sick and confused, so she told her to rest and then they would talk again. Anne slept for the rest of the day and woke up the next morning. It was Saturday and Terry's day off so she just waited for her new friend to get up. When Anne woke up she had a little breakfast and they both sat at the kitchen table and talked. Terry found out little from Anne except that she was in some sort of trouble. She readily assumed that it was with the police, but she could tell that this girl was not a criminal, so she was not worried about harboring her. She had looked through her purse during the night and found identification, not knowing that it was not Anne's.

"So your name is Helen Mack." Anne realized that Terry had found something in the purse with a name on it so she went along with the impersonation.

"Are you in trouble with the police?"

"No." she said but she was not convincing to Terry.

"Never mind, you can stay with me and I"ll get you a job if you want." "I'm leaving the café and starting with the hotel up the street from the golf course. I think I could get you in there with me."

"I have to go for an interview this morning and if I get the job, I'll recommend that they hire you too, okay?"Anne nodded and they finished their coffee and Terry got dressed for her interview.

Anne went and laid down in the living room and watched TV, while Terry got dressed. When Terry came out of the bathroom, he saw Anne dozing on the couch. She turned off the TV and was about to leave for her interview, when she realized that there was nothing for supper that night. Her money was low too. She had paid her rent and pay day at the café was Monday.

"She won't mind." she thought and reached into the purse. There was only a pound and some change. There was an American Express card so she took the card and decided to put it through an ATM.

"I'll just take out five pounds.

"And then I can pay her back on payday."Terry found an ATM machine on Main Street, a couple of blocks from her interview. She ran the card through the machine and being early for her interview, she stopped in the local butcher shop, where she knew Tom, the butcher. She asked him to cut some Lamb chops for her and she would pick them up after her interview.

CHAPTER XXXVII

"Do you want to go to a police golf tournament that I'm running this week?"said Hector Thomson.

"I don't know, I.."

"Look, I've got my best men working on finding Anne."

"In the mean time why don't we relax for a couple of days up in St. Andrews."

"St. Andrews, I don't know, that's where I first met Anne." said Jim.

"Okay, I'll go with you, when do we leave?"

"Tomorrow, we go up there and the tournament is the next day on the "old course"

"We'll have a swell time and you'll meet some of the police from up in Fife and Aberdeen and some of the other small towns in Scotland."

Hector picked up Jim early the next day and they drove north to St. Andrews. They checked into the hotel near the course, had dinner in the restaurant, a couple of drinks and then retired for the evening. They signed in at the tournament desk at 8:00 A.M. Jim got his bag of goodies from the tournament committee. It included some tees, a sleeve of balls and a very nice wind shirt with the St.

Andrews logo on it. Then he and Hector went into the club house and had the continental breakfast which was set up for the golfers. They would tee off at 9:00 A.M. They had time to hit a "bucket" of balls before starting out.

Hector and Jim were paired with two constables from Dundee. Both of these fellows were well over six feet and looked like they could hit. It had the makings of a nice day. There was a clear sky and very little wind.

Terry actually walked by the golf course on her way to the interview, which was at the hotel one block from St. Andrews. She stopped to say hello to Sean, the town constable, who was pushing his golf bag towards the first tee.

"Hey Sean, no cheating."

"You know we police officers never cheat on our wives or at golf."

"Yeah and I"ll sell you the London Bridge for a pound, too." she said.

They both laughed. She liked Sean. He would stop in the café for tea and talk about his kids with her.

"Where are you headed, Terry?

"Going for an interview at the hotel lounge."

"Not going to quit your job at the café, are you?"

"No this would just be waitressing on the weekends.

"Oh, well good luck, mention my name if you need a reference."

"Thanks, Sean, hit 'em straight." Terry thought maybe if she had the time she would have spoken to him about her tenant, but maybe later. The tournament got underway and Jim and Hector hit off and were laughing and teasing each other about their shots, both of which had gone into the rough.

"I belong to Glasgow, dear old Glasgow town, What's the matter with Glasgow, cause it's going round and round." Hector sang and Jim joined in as they walked to their shots.

CHAPTER XXXVIII

Billy McMenemy was a Detective assigned to Hector Thomson. He pulled his car into the parking lot of the golf course. He went to the club house and asked if any of the committee were around.

"Go to the lounge, they are serving tea and scones at the turn for the players. The turn was the ninth hole. There should be some of the committee in there." said a worker in the Pro shop.

Billy was told that Hector and Jim had just had their tea and should be somewhere on the tenth hole. "How can I get there?"

"I'll take you there Inspector." said one of the golf caddies. They jumped into a golf cart and took off for the tenth hole.

Billy saw them on the tenth green. Hector was about to putt, when he looked up and saw the cart approaching.

"What's up, Bill, something important I hope, I'm about to par this hole."

"I need to talk to you, Chief."

There was a lavatory which was a small house near the tenth hole. They went over to it and talked privately, while the foursome finished up the hole.

"Tell the next foursome to pass us up," yelled Hector. Hector and Billy talked for about fifteen minutes and then Billy got back in the cart and drove off with the golf caddy.

Hector took Jim by the hand and led him aside from the foursome.

"Jim we have to go in, we"re finished for the day."

"What are you talking about?"

"Just listen to me and do what I say." said Hector.

"Excuse me gentlemen, we have to leave you, something important has come up."

Hector took Jim off the course to the local hotel lounge.

"Jim, we got some news and I wanted to tell you as soon as possible."

"My man, Billy told me that a woman in London reported the loss of her purse a couple of days ago and they did the usual thing, her name was put in the system in case any of her belongings turned up, like her credit cards ."

"Well, it was a small thing except that she told the Detectives that she had spent the day at the Shady Rest Nursing Home that day she had lost her purse with some credit cards and cash either at the home or on the bus. When we heard Shady Rest Nursing Home it raised a flag about the case of our missing patient, Anne Fulton."

"The complainant was interviewed again and she told our Detectives about riding on the bus with a young lady who seemed "out of sorts" as she put it. Her description fit Anne to a tee."

"Now her American Express Card turned up as being used today and guess where?"Jim looked at him and asked "Where?" " Here, in St. Andrews." "We are waiting for the photo from the ATM machine, which might identify the user."

"Come with me, we are going to wait at the local station." They waited in the station until one of the local Detectives came in with the photo taken off of the ATM camera. "You're not going to believe this, it's Terry Murphy, the waitress at the café."

"She was talking to Sean, just this morning before we teed off." said one of the Detectives.

"Get Sean and see if he knows where she might be." said the Chief Constable.

Sean left his clubs and walked over to the hotel, which was just a block away, where Terry was taking her interview. He asked for the Manager of the Lounge and was told that he was busy showing a new employee the bar and explaining things like inventory and their new money register. He walked into the lounge as the Manager was showing Terry the register. She turned toward him.

"Sean, what are you doing here?"

"I have to talk to you Terry. Is she finished with her interview?"

"Yes, we're all done, so you can start Saturday evening, okay?"

"Yes, that's fine, bye now." Sean walked out with Terry and he asked her to get in his car.

"What's it all about, Sean." "I need to ask you a few questions officially, Ter." "We are just going over to the station." She became uncomfortable now and wondered if it had anything to do with Helen Mack.

Terry sat down in an interview room and Sean introduced Hector Thomson and Jim Feron to her.

"Terry you used an American Express card this morning." "I, I...".

"There's no sense denying it, because we have you on film."

"Okay, I did, but it was only a few pounds and I was going to pay it back." she said.

"It's not that Terry, the card was taken or lost back in London."

Just then Terry realized that the woman in her flat was not Helen Mack. Sean asked her where she got the card. "I found it."

"No, you didn't." said Sean.

"Are you shielding someone?" "We think this card was taken by a patient from the Shady Rest Nursing Home. This patient has mental problems and we are trying to find her." Jim spoke to her and asked

"Miss Murphy, this woman is sick and she is very important to me, we need to find her to bring her back for more treatment."

"If you tell us where she is, I think that we can arrange to drop any charges against you for using the card."

"She's at my flat." "I'll take you there." They all got in the police cruiser and went to Terry's flat.

They went upstairs to Terry's flat and she unlocked the door. They walked in and Terry called out "Miss Mack, Helen, where are you?" She was not anywhere in sight. A pile of clothes lay on the couch. "She's gone." said Terry. Jim's heart dropped down to his shoes.

Then all of a sudden, Anne came out of the bathroom. She had taken a shower and was wearing a robe.

"I hope you don't mind, I took the liberty of taking your robe to wear."

She was drying her hair when she saw the group in front of her. Jim, Hector and Terry stood there without saying a word. She looked at Terry first then, her eyes drifted toward the men, Hector, then Jim. She collapsed in front of them and Hector grabbed for her before she hit the floor. Then they put her on the couch and Terry got a cold towel to put on her face.

"Anne, Anne, it's me Jim." She opened her eyes very slowly and looked at Jim. "Jim, I was trying to see you off at the plane and something ran into me and then I don't remember..." Jim smiled at her. She had gone back in her mind to when she was hurt. It was a good sign. They took her back to the Shady Rest and after a few days the doctor agreed to release her. She had improved to where she remembered Jim and her former life. There were huge gaps from the time of her accident, which would probably never surface.

Jim began to court her as he wanted to when they first met. They went to dinner, shows, and fell in love all over again. Jim asked her to marry him and she said yes. They would be married in England and plans were made for Jim's family to come over for the wedding. Alex would come and Tom Bragg and his wife were invited and they were coming. Even William Colin agreed to come.

They would have their reception at the Le Meridien Grovesnor Hotel.

The wedding was held in St. Andrews because that's where they met and it had so much significance to both of them. The day before the wedding Jim picked up the London Times and read something that drove him almost to distraction.

"RETIRED DETECTIVE INVOLVED IN TRACKING Bin Laden TO BE MARRIED IN ST. ANDREWS."

" Where the hell did they get this information" he said to himself".

"This is not good." He got on the phone and called Colin in Washington. Colin was also furious about the leak to the press, especially linking Jim to the attempt to capture Bin Laden. It made him a target for Al Qu'aida and they both knew it.

"Where did they get this information." he asked Bill.

"I have men working on it and I do believe it came out of Congress."

"Believe me

Jim, I'll have their ass if I can zero in on who let this out to the press."

"I have a strong suspicion, but I can't prove it right now." "God help them if I do."

"I am sincerely sorry about this." "Will you be coming to the wedding?"

"Wouldn't miss it for the world. You guys have done so much for me and this country. I almost got the President to come, but he is so tied up right now... Anyway he sends his blessings and he is sending you a special Wedding gift."

Jim could not find words about the President's concern and his gift. It was such an honor and he appreciated it.

The wedding was held in St. James Roman Catholic Church. Jim's daughter was the Maid of Honor. He had an awful time deciding on who his best man was to be. That was decided by Tom Bragg, who told Jim that it would be unthinkable for him to choose anyone other than Alex. Alex invited his girl friend from Virginia and he paid her fare over. He was really smitten with her and it was apparent from the way he hovered over her from the time she arrived.

The wedding ceremony was an hour but no one minded because it was so beautiful. Anne was a vision in her wedding dress and Jim looked very distinguished in his blue tuxedo.

After they said their vows and were pronounced "Man and Wife". They turned toward each other and kissed and then everyone clapped. They went to the front of the church where they met with all of the visitors who came on line to wish them congratulations. After they came out of the lobby, they were bombarded with a hail of rice from all directions. Anne went first down the steps toward the limousine, followed by Jim, who was a few steps behind.

The black car somehow had gotten a parking space in front of the limousine. No one seemed disturbed by it's presence. As if in a scene from the past, a man emerged from the car and approached Jim from behind. He never got within five feet of him though before a big black Security Agent intercepted him. He smashed the man in the face with a right cross and broke his nose. There was a screech of wheels as two cars came down the street and blocked the car with the other kidnappers. Four men leaped out of these cars and pointed automatic rifles at the windows, all of the windows. The men inside didn't have a chance to even move, because they were surrounded so swiftly. The Security men opened the car door and as one of them grabbed the kidnappers he said

"Are you for the bride or the groom." The kidnappers were pulled out of the car, not too gently and forced face down on the ground, where they were handcuffed and taken away.

William Colin went over to Jim and Anne and made sure that they were both okay.

"I couldn't take any chances after that article appeared in the newspaper." he said.

"So I had some of my Security people on hand."

"Thank you, Bill, Let's get to the reception hall and have some champagne."

CHAPTER XXXIX

Anne and Jim had an outside room on the QEII. It was their honeymoon trip. They spent the days in the various pubs on board. The Yacht club, The Lion Bar, whatever pub had music soft and mellow to listen to while they sipped their cocktails.

The ocean was smooth and blue. Jim got up each morning and went to the Spa, while Anne called for the steward and got her early morning tea. Then when Jim returned they dressed and went to breakfast.

It was after lunch and they were standing on the desk looking out over the ocean. It was a beautiful day, the sun was warm and the water was calm. Anne was the first to see it. A small ship was about three hundred yards astern of the ship. She wasn't quite sure what it was, but when she told Jim and he looked out in the direction she told him, he wasn't quite sure what it was.

"It looks like a Sub Chaser." He said.

"I saw a picture of one when the USS Pueblo was hi-jacked by the North Koreans back in 1968"

The ship maneuvered itself into position and then with one of it's 25mm Guns it fired a shot across the bow of the QEII.

"What the hell do they thing they're doing." said the Captain, who was called to the bridge upon the sighting of the craft.

The Sub Chaser started to flash a message to the big ship.

"Heave to and prepare to be boarded."

"Heave to or the next time we fire directly at your ship."

The Captain ordered the engine room to slow down but not stop. The big ship moved very slowly, somewhat hardly noticeably. The Sub Chaser seemed satisfied that the QE II was not attempting to escape so they settled for the very slow speed that the ship had reduces itself to.

A small tender approached the ship. It had five men aboard and they were armed with AK47 rifles. They climbed aboard and demanded to see the Captain.

A ship's officer led them to a cabin, which was located near the bridge. The one who was the leader marched in front of the group and he entered the cabin first. The cabin was a luxurious one with a portion fitted out as an office, with a desk and computer. As they entered a man in a uniform was seated at the computer with his back to the door.

"Captain, these gentlemen are here to speak with you." He never turned around but continued on with his work on the computer.

"Yes, what can I do for you." he said in a very blasé manner. "We have come to take one of your passengers." "Oh, is that what you want?"

"Yes, you will surrender Mr. Feron and his bride to us or we will blow your ship out of the water."The Captain turned around and faced the men with the guns.

"Have your men wait outside the cabin, I would like to talk to you alone, sir."

The leader ordered his men to step outside.

"Yes, are you going to comply or do I signal our ship to start firing?"

"Let me introduce myself to you, Mr. Mohammed or Singh or whatever your fucking name is."

"I am Major Bragg of the United States Marine Corps and you and your slime balls are all under arrest."Bragg drew a .45 Automatic from his waist which had been hidden when he was seated. The leader called out to his men who were outside but there was no answer. "They are being led to their new accommodations, sir as you will also. The leader was taken out of the cabin by a couple of burly Marines and disarmed.

Bragg and his Marines quickly dressed up in the hi-jackers clothes and got into the tender to return to the sub-chaser. First a message was flashed to the Sub Chaser.

"Mission Accomplished, We have our prisoners and are returning. The tender pulled alongside of the Sub Chaser and the "passengers" were observed boarding. After a half an hour, the "passengers" were observed leaving the Sub Chaser and boarding the tender again headed back to the QEII. Just about the time that they came alongside of the Queen, a huge explosion ripped the Sub Chaser and within minutes she capsized and sank.

Tom Bragg and his men and the "imposters" made to look like a man and woman entered the Captain's cabin, where the Captain, Jim and Anne were all waiting.

"They had some kind of an accident on board. So we left. Someone accidentally lit a fuse attached to plastic explosives and left it in the hold. Too bad."

Tom was very cold and calculating about the destruction of the hi-jacker's ship.

"They didn't take too well to our little deception " " We had to disarm everyone and then we offered them the chance to become prisoners, however they preferred to die for the cause. So we didn't argue, it would have been a little crowded on the tender anyway. As they spoke a flight of F-18's passed over head.

"Oh, I forgot to tell you, Jim, your son called on the radio and told us they were tracking the ship which had intercepted the Queen and a flight of F-18's were sent to take them out."

"It seems "Investicom" was keeping an eye on the QEII at the request of William Colin." "So you see we had all the bases covered."

Jim just smiled and shook his head and held Anne's hand.

CHAPTER XXXX

Ten years had past since Jim and Anne were married and almost kidnapped by Al Q'uaida. They had nine very happy years together when one night Anne went to sleep and didn't wake up.

Jim remained in the house alone. He was fully retired from his second job with the government. His son and daughter had taken over "Investicom". Alex went on to marry Virginia and they moved to Virginia. He too had retired. He kept in touch with Jim by phone and e-mail and occasionally would come up to visit. Jim was now a grandfather by his son and daughter. They would keep tabs on him and his health, calling every day or stopping by to see him. He was content to live in his home and he would still take on assignments from one of the local priests, Father Nolan who would ask him to help find a biological parent or sibling. He took on these tasks as a sort of hobby, but he derived great satisfaction in helping people reunite with their families.

The world of law enforcement had changed in the last ten years. Some new innovations had been added. A couple of the new programs that were added were all convicts had a implanted chip put inside their bodies. This chip enabled released felons to be tracked from a giant computer. Their whereabouts and activities were closely monitored. If they had any ideas about committing a crime after their release they were soon to find out that they would be found and rearrested. Of course the American Civil Liberties Union and several liberal groups fought very hard to prevent this procedure, but a volunteer test program proved so successful that Congress enacted a bill and the President passed it. The crime rate was cut in half as a result. Another innovation was the installation of sensors in private homes that would determine if anyone came onto the property who was not a resident or a family member.

Once this was determined it activated a camera and if any attempts were made to break in, it notified a central station monitor and the police. But in addition it formed an electric ring around the property preventing the person from leaving the grounds. It would shock anyone leaving such as a stun gun would.

Another great innovation was a track set up on the highways off the shoulder of the road. It would transport an injured person who had either been in a car wreck or someone who just had a heart attack or was otherwise disabled. The injured or sick person would be placed inside the capsule, which was on the track and mechanically given oxygen or an IV and then transported to the nearest hospital.

Also on the highways, sensors were being installed as an experiment that had the power to slow down automobiles that were going to fast. It worked like cruise control and in one highway it reduced the number of accidents considerably.

These were only a few of the new additions to law enforcement. Police cruisers were much more advanced with individual computers in every car. There were many other innovations in the police cruisers. They could attain speeds of 80 miles per hour in less than four seconds. They had superior steering capabilities. They could make an almost ninety degree turn with only minimal deceleration. They had radio communications capable of communicating with any police agency in the United States.

Jim's life was very quiet except for the work he did for the church finding people for no charge. He relished in his ability to help people. He received regular visits from Father Nolan, Catholic Priest, Father Wisbauer, Episcopalian Minister and Rabbi Schiffer.

He had built a smaller version of "Investicom" without all the Top Secret programs, which he used to trace people. He accepted no fees for his work. He asked only that if he was successful, which he was in a lot of cases, that the person or persons donate money to their respective churches or temples. Every morning Jim would take a walk into town. He stopped at the local diner on Main Street and had a big breakfast. Before he sat down to eat he would buy a newspaper and read it while he had his meal.

This one morning he passed a police cruiser parked outside. Inside he saw a police officer that he knew seated at the counter. "Hi Tim." he said. "How's Dad?" Jim had known Tim's father who was a retired Suffolk County Detective. "He's doing alright. He's back playing golf again after the by-pass he had." "That's great. Tell him I was asking for him." "I will" and Tim ordered a roll and coffee as Jim hunted for a booth. Jim had his breakfast and read his paper. The headline read "Kenya develops Atomic Bomb" "Threatens Nigeria and other African countries"

"That's great" he thought. "We had enough trouble with North Korea back in 2003. Jim finished his breakfast and walked outside the diner. Tim, the Suffolk County Police Officer was sitting his cruiser. Across the street a woman was walking her baby down Main Street.

Tim waved to Jim and he went over to the cruiser. "Nice car." said Jim.

"Get in and sit down." said Tim. "I want to show some of our new gadgets." " This is our computer, over here our Global Positioning System. Tim went over all of the devices with Jim."God, the first radio car I ever rode in only had a one way radio. We could receive but not send."

As they sat and discussed the cruiser's complex electronic systems, a car came down the street and pulled in at the curb just a few feet in front of the woman with the baby carriage.

The car pulled alongside the woman and it appeared that someone in the car was asking her for directions. She poked her head inside of the window and was answering some sort of question. The driver, a man exited the car and came around the back of the car. He pushed the woman to the ground and grabbed the baby. He then circled back into the car and the car sped off. The woman stunned for the moment screamed and Tim and Jim looked in her direction and saw the car escaping down Main Street. Jim pulled his cruiser out of the parking lot of the diner and pulled alongside the woman. "They took my baby." and she pointed to the car racing up the street. Tim didn't hesitate. He pounced on the accelerator. Then he screeched to a stop.

"Get out of the car, Jim". Jim hesitated and he didn't move fast enough so Tim said

"Put you seat belt on." "We're after them." Jim buckled himself in and the cruiser took off like a rocket. The cruiser reached a speed of 80 miles an hour inside of seconds.

The getaway car had a good lead and was already a couple of hundred yards away.

The cruiser was now picking up speed and approaching a car in traffic. Jim did what most passengers would do he stepped on the brake. "the imaginary brake" as they came upon the car in front of them. Tim put his hand on the transmission control and pushed it into "Horizontal". The wheels came up and a set of wheels in the center of the undercarriage came down pushing the car horizontally and then he hit the control again and the wheels came down and the car proceeded straight. What happened was the car approached a car in front of it and his control moved the car to the right of that car and then straight so it could pass. The "G" force of what he did was not a factor because it was all done so swiftly. Jim was amazed at the control Tim had with his cruiser. The cruiser was now gaining on the kidnappers. They were on the Sunrise Highway passing Hospital Road, which became a two lane highway. Tim had radioed ahead and a Helicopter passed overhead and passed the kidnappers. The Helicopter got to a point where it was far enough ahead of the kidnapers and when it did it landed on the highway.

The Helicopter enacted an electrical shield across the highway. Another new innovation that the new law enforcement had. As the kidnapper's car passed the electrical shield, it's system shut down and all it could do was coast. The driver realizing that he had no power, stopped the car and both he and his female partner jumped out and ran into the woods off of he highway. Tim pulled up behind them and got out of the cruiser and started after them along with some officers from the Helicopter. Jim got out of the car and watched. He felt a pain in his chest and sank to his knees. He held his chest as he walked over to the kidnappers car. He reached in and took out the baby. He held her in his arms and she looked up at him and a little smile crossed her face. The pain in his chest got more intense and he sat down with the baby in his arms. Then he passed out. When he woke up he was in a hospital bed and an IV was in his arm. A young nurse was by his side. "Mr. Feron, you had a little heart attack, we are monitoring you and we think you ill be alright, but you will stay over night."

Jim rested easily. He looked around his room. He was not alone. There was an elderly gentleman in the bed across the room. He was very pale and his eyes were closed. Jim just closed his eyes and went to sleep.

CHAPTER XXXX

When Jim woke up, he looked over at the elderly gentleman, who was awake and staring at him. "Hi, my name is Frank McCarthy." Jim introduced himself and they started to talk. Frank was very friendly but it was clear that he was a sick man. The conversation led to family's associations. Jim learned that Frank was a retired fireman and had contracted a lung disease while working on the World Trade Center tragedy. "That was a long time ago and now I'm paying for it." he said. "Never the less, I'd do it all over again. We found over two dozen bodies but the most gratifying day of my life was the day we found a pocket under the rubble where a young uniformed cop was buried and he was still alive."

Jim found out that Frank had only a few weeks to live. He found out quite by accident. He was walking in the hospital corridor and overheard one of the doctors speaking to a nurse. "When his family comes to visit, ask them to call me. I'm going to have to break the news to them and I don't want him to know."

Jim returned to his room and sat down next to Frank. Frank was very interested in some of Jim's "war stories" about the Police Department and "Investicom"

"You must be pretty good at locating people. I guess." "You might say that."said Jim. "I wonder if, nah, never mind...." "What were you going to say?" asked Jim."I don't want to impose. I know that I'm a pretty sick fella and maybe I don't have too long.""I had or have a sister, who I haven't seen in ten years. We had a little falling out over something stupid and she left New York. I would really like to find her. I thought maybe since you are so good at finding people, maybe you could find her for me."

Jim nodded. "Give me what information you have about her, date of birth, social security number, whatever you have." When Jim's son and daughter came to visit, he gave them the information n Frank's sister. "This is a special job. Do your best." "Piece of cake." said Jim's son.

A day later, Jim was taking his usual stroll down the corridor. His son, John got off the elevator and he had a woman with him. "Dad, This is Maureen McCarthy, She is Frank's sister. I found her through "Investicom" and when I called her she immediately flew here from Pittsburgh." Jim introduced himself and said "I'm so glad to meet you. Frank will be thrilled."As they walked toward the room they all saw a team heading very quickly towards the room with an emergency cart. Jim told John and Maureen to stay down the hall, while he investigated. He got to the room in time to observe a doctor and two nurses working on his room mate. "He's dead." said the doctor. He pulled the defibrillator off of the patient's chest. Jim grabbed the doctor by therm. "Try again." "It's no use, he's gone." "Maybe you didn't hear me, I said try it again." Jim squeezed the doctor's arm and looked right into his eyes. The doctor applied the defibrillator again. There was no response. Again he tried and this time they got a blip on the screen. Then it got stronger. "He's back, but I don't think he'll last long." said the doctor. Jim went out to the hall and got Frank's sister. "You haven't got much time." She went in and Frank opened his eyes and reached for her hand. "I'm sorry." he said. "Never mind Frank. It's all right."

He smiled and then closed his eyes.

Jim was released from the hospital the next day and instead of being picked up by his children, he asked that he simply leave the hospital on his own and meet them later for lunch. He walked out of the hospital and breathed the fresh air. He took a deep breath. He thought about Frank and a tear came to his eye. He thought "At least he got to see his sister." Frank's sister had thanked him profusely for finding her and giving them both the opportunity to be together before he died.

What was next for him. The whole world of law enforcement had changed and a lot of it was due to "Investicom".

CHAPTER XXXXI

Jim was called one day by his son. He wanted him to come over to the laboratory. They were having a problem with "Investicom". It was a critical situation.

"Dad, I'm worried that maybe we , I mean the computer has contracted a virus."

"Several of our programs have gone haywire. Can you come over as soon as possible. I thought since you worked this thing for so many years, that maybe you have some suggestions. We have not been able to clear up this situation for two days."

"John, I will be there this afternoon. Have you tried to contact Alex?"

"Yes we have and he is not that far from the laboratory. He will be here when you arrive." Jim thought pleasantly of a reunion with Alex, but he wished it would have been under more favorable conditions. Anyway, he was determined that he and Alex would solve what was wrong with the computer. Jim's sons tone was worrisome. He thought to himself. "Has someone finally found a way to mess up this computer." Over the years, it had solved numerouscases, found thousands of missing persons and performed a multitude of services to the United States Government and it's Allies. Jim got into his car and headed to the airport in Islip. He would grab a shuttle flight to Washington, D.C. The flight left at 10 in the morning. The flight was only forty minutes long. He would be at the laboratory before noon.

The flight however short gave him time to reflect over the years, the vast accomplishments that "Investicom" had accomplished.

He thought of the search for Osama Bin Laden and how he and Tom Bragg had gone to Pakistan and into the mountains looking for Osama's hideout. Osama had died in 2003. He died of kidney failure. His body had been secretly buried by some of the Al Q'uaida. They were afraid that his enemies would mutilate it as was done to Mussolini in World War II.

Sadam Hussein stopped being a problem also in 2003.

Another one of the problems of the day were the North Koreans, who finally agreed to terminate their Nuclear Program in return for economic aid in the way of food and fuel. However, the shipments of food were controlled by the government.

The North Korean government decided that they would only give out food packages to their Military Personnel. This resulted in riots. The men in the military rebelled when they found that their loved ones were starving while food was available and only given to the Military in order to maintain a huge armed force. The revolt resulted in the overthrow of the Communist Government and a new Democratic leadership took over, which immediately initiated negotiations with the South to normalize all relations and put the country on an equal footing.

He remembered the initial cases involving the kidnappings and the assistance they gave to the New York City Police and the FBI.

The attempted assassination of the President and the Pope was one of the greatest achievements that the computer had ever contributed to law enforcement.

Then he thought of Anne and their happy years together. He thought to himself of how the computer had helped solve the disappearance of his first wife. How it helped reunite him with his children. It was like a member of his family.

The plane started to descend and the announcement to fasten seat belts was given. He looked out the port window in time to see the Capitol Dome.

"It's still a beautiful sight." he thought. He walked through the airport toward the taxi and limousine area, but on his way a black suited gentleman was holding up a sign "Feron" and he knew that they had dispatched a car for him.

CHAPTER XXXXII

The Limo arrived at Quantico Marine base , where the laboratory had been established. They arrived after only a twenty-five minute ride. The driver told Jim that he would take his suitcase to the Hilton Hotel in Washington. D.C. Where accommodations had been arranged for him. He thanked the driver gave him a tip and took his briefcase and went to the gate of the Lab. He passed through the security. It had all been arranged for his entry.

A jeep picked him up and a Marine Sergeant drove him to the lab site. He hopped out of the jeep and went to the lab door. The Marine Sergeant stepped in front of him and placed a plastic card into a slot and the door unlatched.

They walked down a corridor which led to another door which had to be unlocked also by a plastic card. "God, how many doors do we need to pass through."

"Sorry, sir, Security you know."

There was his son approaching him. He had a very somber look on his face.

"Dad" "I'm glad to see you. We got big problems, here." All of a sudden he saw another old familiar face. One he hadn't seen in a couple of years. "Alex, you old son of a gun."

Alex and Jim hugged one another. Alex gave him a kiss on the cheek. "I've missed you." "Yeah, we haven't seen each other since Anne's funeral."

"Yes, my friend and how are you. You had a little bout with the heart I heard." "Yeah, but I'm fine now." "Have you figured out anything about this new trouble with "Investicom"?

"No, I'm puzzled, It doesn't seem to be a virus, but it acts like one." Jim was anxious to take a look at the computer to see if there was anything he could help to solve the problem. "Look", first we are going to have a little lunch break. You couldn't have had a chance to eat anything flying in from Long Island as soon as I contacted you. "Okay, If there's nothing pressing right now, I guess I could stand a bite."

A tray of Corned Beef Sandwiches were brought in and a six pack of beer. They all sat at a kind of picnic table and enjoyed the meal along with some lively conversation about the old days.

"Where'd you get these sandwiches, they taste just like the ones we used to get in the city, remember, what was the name of that place?"

"It was Katz's Dad." "That's the name of the place."

"They had this big sign on the wall. Send a Salami to your boy in the Army." "And those franks and the french fries were home made." They laughed and finished their lunch.

"Okay, let's go in and see if we can fix the old girl." said Jim. Jim sat down at the keyboard and attempted to enter a command. The big computer made a whizzing sound and lights flashed and then the printer started up and a sheaf of paper came out. It was attempting to answer Jim's command. "What did you ask it to do, Dad?" said John. "I asked it to give me a list of DNA Identification networks in New York State"

They went over to the printer and Jim tore off the sheet with the information. "What kind of crap is this?" he asked. The sheet had a page of x's and o's. "Hugs and kisses, I get." "Well let's take a look at the insides of this old girl."

They unscrewed a panel which had a maze of motherboards, Video cards, memory, motherboards, and all the complicated components that made up a computer of this magnitude.   They checked parts and replaced some of which they thought had a flaw, but no matter what they did, the computer would not function. They worked on the computer for over an hour, but nothing they tried worked.

After working on it for an hour, Jim's son John came in and told them that a "super technician" had been called and was on his way to help them. Jim and Alex were a little disappointed that they could not solve the problem and that some "super technician" was coming to solve the problem, but they would wait and maybe this person had the expertise that they lacked.

The expert arrived soon after they were told . He was a strange looking man and they stared at his get up. He had a beard, long hair and was dressed like a "Hippy". Alex whispered to Jim "This guy's going to fix Investicom" "This I have to see." Jim just stared at the man and shook his head.

The expert went to the keyboard and entered several commands. The big computer did not respond. On the computer was an abort switch, which was only to be used in a case where the computer was shorting out and overheating and in danger of burning up. He went toward the switch. "What are you doing?" said Alex. "I am going to hit the abort switch." he replied. "Don't do that, that will cause irreparable damage to the computer."

Never the less he was at the switch in a second and pulled the lever. Now the big computer started to make an unusual sound.

Then it happened, first sparks and then an explosion of light and sound. Jim stepped forward. He did not see the others moving back. He stood alone in front of the computer. The computer noises and sparks suddenly changed. The sparks became a series of fireworks. "Red, White and Blue" rockets spurted out of the sides of "Investicom".

The music was your basic John Phillip Sousa. First came the Stars and Stripes forever, followed by a combination of Sousa favorites. Jim's mouth just dropped open and all he could do was stare at the display. "What the f------" he started to say and then he turned around to see what was going on behind him. Behind him was Alex, his children and then some people he hadn't seen for a while. There was Tom Bragg, now a General, standing alongside of newly elected Senator William Colin from the state of Virginia. And a whole host of military brass, some of whom Jim remembered from the campaign in Afghanistan searching for Osama Bin Laden. There were other men and women in suits who were from the Pentagon and had been involved in the administration of the big computer over the years. Jim looked into the crowd and he saw an old familiar face. Hector Thomson. He hadn't seen Hector since the death of Anne. Hector had come from England just for the funeral. "Hello, dear friend." said Jim and they hugged.

They were all smiling at Jim and then they started to applaud. Tom Bragg broke out in song "For he's a jolly good fellow, for he's a jolly good fellow" and they all joined in. Jim realized what was going on. It was all a ruse to get him to the laboratory and then he saw what had been hidden in the corner behind a screen. There was a bar set up and trays of food of steak and lobster and shrimp and pasta. "We had to figure a way to get you here." Jim shook hands with Colin and hugged Tom Bragg.

"I've never hugged a General before." He noticed a tear in his eye. They had a few drinks and everyone filled their plats with food and then Colin got up and made an announcement. "We didn't do all this just so we could have a party." "I have a presentation to make to Jim Feron and Alex for their years of service to their country. But before I do that, we are waiting for an honored guest to arrive About that time there was a sound of sirens outside the building and several black limousines pulled up.

There was no mistaking who the man was that entered the room. He walked over to Jim and Alex and shook their hands. I'm sorry that I'm late for the festivities, but perhaps you'll both have a sip of champagne with me. But first we have a presentation to make and I would prefer that Senator Colin make it, because he has been such an integral part of the "Investicom" project."

With that Senator Colin asked Jim and Alex to come forward and he was handed two boxes from which he took two medals. He proceeded to pin the medals on both of them. "These are Presidential Medals of Honor and the inscription reads "For Service to the United States at great sacrifice and above and beyond the call of duty. Once the medals were pinned on, all of the people in the room applauded and came forward to congratulate Jim and Alex. The first to come forward was the President. Senator Colin then filled all of the glasses and the President pointed his glass at the two men and made his toast. "Here's to our country and our flag and all the best things that they stand for." "Here, here" they all said. The party was about to end when Colin took Jim by the hand and led him to little old lady who had been in the crowd. He introduced her to Jim and she said "You probably don't remember me." "I came to you a number of years ago and asked you if you could find my father who was in the Marine Corps and was stationed in New Zealand during World War II."

"You found him for me. He was in Baltimore living with another old retiree" "We had a reunion in Arizona about six months later. He came back to New Zealand with me and lived with me for another ten years before he died. I can't thank you enough for those ten years. It was the happiest of my life." "This is my Grandson." "How do you do sir, I'm very pleased to have met you." "It's my pleasure." said Jim. Then they said Goodbye and went out the door. "I thought you would enjoy meeting these people." said Colin.

The celebration and the dedication was over now and everyone said their goodbyes and all went their separate ways. General Bragg back to Quantico, Va., Alex with his wife Virginia said their goodbyes and reminded Jim that he was welcome at their home and looked forward to him and his family visiting, which Jim promised to do. Senator Colin left with the President after shaking everyone's hands and wishing them well.

Jim and his children were among the last to leave. A limousine took Jim to the airport and within three hours he was riding back to his home in Long Island. It had been a great day.

EPILOGUE

This story was totally fiction and the characters are fiction as well. Some of the material used in this book was gleaned from articles written about Osama Bin Laden; Afghanistan; the United States Marine Corps; the Kennedy Assassination; the gas attack on the Tokyo Subway system. A lot of the technical knowledge was taken from magazine articles and articles on the Internet. A great portion of the possible use of the computer for law enforcement was part of the writer's imagination. It remains to be seen if a lot of the technology mentioned in this story will come to fruition. The advances of computer technology in the last few years have been so astounding that it is hard to imagine what lies ahead for us. It could become a golden age and one that can promote peace to the world. It can be a boon to the Medical Profession as it already has. We could be heading for a civilization where we don't have to worry about crime or sickness or war. H G Wells wrote about time travel. Even that is not as implausible as it once was. When the writer was born, Space travel was talked of but no one thought that there would ever be a modern Buck Rogers. Who ever imagined that we would have six foot wide flat screen televisions broadcasting events all over the world and from outer space. So the Technology used by "Investicom" may not be so far fetched. Let's see.

FINIS

About the Author

The author is a retired New York City Police Detective/Sergeant. He remembers the day he was sworn in as a New York City Police Officer in February, 1956. He went on to be a Patrolman and a Traffic Officer. From there he was promoted to the Detective Division and worked for 14 years in the Organized Crime Section. He was promoted from Detective Third Grade to 2nd Grade and then to Sergeant. He was selected to work on the theft of the famous "French Connection" narcotics and did so for two years. Then he went to work for Robert Morgenthau's office the New York County District Attorney.

It was during this time that he met Kevin Maher and this association of an informant and a police officer became more like a father and son relationship. They collaborated on many important successful investigations during this time. After serving with the Queens DA, Doherty retired and worked for ten years for the Department of Defense doing background investigations for "Top Secret" clearances. He left there to work for the Suffolk County District Attorney as a Detective Investigator working in several different bureaus. He and Maher at this time along with Charles Kipps wrote a book *Cop Without a Badge*. This book received notoriety during a television show on Bravo called *The Real Housewives of New Jersey*. Jim is now semi-retired and does private investigations for law firms and the federal government. It gives him time to spend with his wife Betty, his six children, Pat, Pam, Betsy, Gerri, Jim and John and their families including his 12 grandchildren, Teresa, Samantha, Christopher, Brittany, Andrew, Caitlin, Jim, Fallon, John, Nicole, Kylie and Michael.

www.ingramcontent.com/pod-product-compliance
Lightning Source LLC
Chambersburg PA
CBHW051232050326
40689CB00007B/895